The Pale-Faced Girl

Cath Hensby Worboys

O&U
Onwards & Upwards

Onwards and Upwards Publishers

4 The Old Smithy, London Road, Rockbeare,
EX5 2EA, United Kingdom.
www.onwardsandupwards.org

First edition, published in the United Kingdom by Onwards and Upwards Publishers Ltd. (2021).

ISBN:	978-1-78815-580-9
Typeface:	Sabon LT
Artist:	APRILILY

This is a work of fiction. Names, characters, businesses, places, events, locales, and incidents are either the products of the author's imagination or used in a fictitious manner. Any resemblance to actual persons, living or dead, or actual events is purely coincidental.

Contents

The Pale-Faced Girl

1

The Pale-Faced Girl

It had not been a good week for Jack. He had failed, again, to get into the school football team. He had been in trouble, and it had all been Harvey Grahams' fault. Grahams had tampered with the equipment in the science lab, but it was Jack who had nearly caused an explosion and filled the room with the most disgusting-smelling gas imaginable. The result: an after school detention. He had been grounded for being rude to his mum, and to top it all, his Xbox was broken.

Saturday arrived, one of those dreary days when the weather seemed undecided – damp and grey and showery. Not that it really mattered, Jack thought gloomily, as he was not allowed out anyway. He wondered what his friends Alfie and Callum were doing today; they were probably over at Alfie's house on his Xbox.

Hour after monotonous hour, the day dragged on. Towards the end of the afternoon his mum sent him out to the corner shop for a few groceries. Usually he would have complained but, as he was grounded, any opportunity to go outside was better than none.

It was still drizzling slightly, but the fresh air was welcome. Jack ambled to the shop, threw the required items into a basket and, on joining the queue for the checkout, noticed a girl ahead whom he did not recognize. She looked about his age, but he did not recall having ever seen her at school. She was unusually striking; her hair, falling below her shoulders, was positively golden, and her face was an almost unearthly white. Jack watched her pay for her goods, pick up her bag and glide towards the door with fluid, graceful movements. She paused at the exit, turned, and looking directly at Jack, winked. The next moment she was gone.

Jack was startled. At twelve years old he was not accustomed to being winked at by girls. He was even more surprised when he left the shop only two minutes later and found no trace of her. There was nowhere the girl could have walked to that was not visible from the shop. Perhaps she had left by car? But Jack was certain that the three cars parked outside had been there when he arrived, and he prided himself on his observational skills. He had not heard any other vehicles pulling into the car park. It was odd. Jack scanned the road ahead, but saw no-one resembling the golden-haired, pale-faced girl. It appeared that she had vanished into thin air.

Puzzled, Jack headed home. Perhaps his mind was playing tricks on him, a bit like an optical illusion. "That's what you get when you're stuck indoors all day," he thought to himself, grimly. He definitely needed to get out more!

2

A Fight

A new week began, and Jack thought no more of his strange encounter with the disappearing girl. After being grounded all weekend it was a relief to return to school on Monday, even though he had to face a detention at the end of the day.

Trudging home that evening, however, Jack thought that the week would never end. His arm ached from writing. To make matters worse, detention had been held by Mrs. Grimshaw, his least favourite teacher. She seemed to take particular delight in keeping him right up until five o'clock.

As Jack approached a narrow lane he was surprised to hear voices. Three figures from his school blocked the path. He immediately recognized the tallest boy as Harvey Grahams, and felt a surge of anger. He had not forgiven him for landing him in detention. The second boy he did not know by name, although he had seen him skulking around with Harvey on occasions – a thin, surly individual. Jack could barely make out the third boy; he appeared to be crouching beside a hedge, hidden from view. He could hear his high-pitched squeals, and drawing closer, Jack realized that the first two boys were kicking him. The blood rushed to his head; he did not know what was going on, but no way was this fair! Jack lunged towards Harvey and tackled him from behind. Startled, Harvey swung around.

"Fletcher! What are you doing here?" he demanded angrily.

"I could ask you the same question," Jack retorted.

"That's none of your business."

"It is when you're picking on someone who can't stand up for themselves."

A whimper emanated from the hedge.

"Shut up, you!" Harvey growled, aiming a kick which was followed by another squeal.

"Leave him alone! What's he done to you?"

"Keep out of it, Fletcher." Harvey took a step towards him.

Jack smiled. "You don't scare me, Grahams. And I haven't forgotten what you did last week either."

As Harvey advanced in the same menacing manner, Jack deftly turned to the side, leaving his foot in place just long enough for the lumbering Harvey to stumble over it and crash headlong to the ground. Jack knelt beside the cowering victim, who glanced up at him with wide, terrified eyes. Jack instantly recognized the boy as Marcus Littlewood, a rather unfortunate individual in his year. Marcus was small and skinny, with ginger hair that stuck out at all angles, but still did not manage to hide his protruding ears. He did not have many friends, and would wander aimlessly around the school, looking somewhat forlorn. He was always the last person to be picked for teams, and was a prime target for a bully. Jack reached out his hand to help him up.

"Jack! Look out!"

Jack swung around, just in time to see the surly boy towering over him, his school bag raised, ready to strike. Jack grinned. Before the boy had a chance to aim the missile at him, Jack grabbed the bag and threw it across the ground. He turned to a quivering Marcus.

"You go on home. Don't worry about these two – I'll sort them out."

"Thanks." Marcus shot Jack a grateful look and ran off without another word. Only then did Jack realize that the cautionary voice had not been Marcus', but a girl's. Yet there was no-one else around.

"Think you're so clever, don't you, Fletcher?" Harvey Grahams had recovered himself, and was now advancing towards Jack, looking furious. The other boy joined him, his face surlier than ever.

"You just can't keep your nose out of other people's business, can you?" Harvey gave Jack a hard push. Jack stumbled backwards, but managed to regain his balance, and stood as tall as he could. Both boys towered over him, and Harvey must have been twice his weight. He was not going to let them intimidate him, though, no way.

"And what were you doing, picking on someone like Marcus Littlewood?" he flashed back angrily. "What's your problem – too scared to fight people your own size?"

"I'd shut your mouth if I were you." Harvey almost spat out the words.

"Gonna make me?"

They were closing in on him, backing him into a thick hedge. He looked around frantically, but there was no means of escape. He did not stand a chance against them. The boys seemed to sense his panic. They were leering unpleasantly.

"Not quite so gobby now, are we, Fletcher?" Harvey grabbed his shoulders and thrust him backwards. Jack's head hit something hard, probably a tree trunk. The next second he was doubling up as a punch landed in his stomach. Then he was being kicked in the shins. Jack tried to fight back, but it was hopeless. How could he possibly beat these two louts?

Another punch in the stomach winded him, and he leant forward, gasping for breath. Suddenly, he glimpsed a movement out of the corner of his eye. Turning surreptitiously, he saw a white hand waving from somewhere inside the hedge.

A voice hissed, "Jack! Jack! Over here!"

It was the same voice as earlier.

Jack did not have time to think. Harvey and his sidekick were bearing down on him once again, looking as though they intended to finish him off once and for all. Jack dived sideways into the hedge, grabbed the outstretched hand, and felt himself being pulled backwards. He heard a resounding thud as the two boys aimed a punch at him simultaneously, missed, as he retreated into the hedge, and collided with each other. Then everything turned black.

Jack opened his eyes to find himself sitting on a grassy bank. He blinked, his eyes adjusting to the daylight. His head was pounding. He blinked again, realizing that he was not alone, and then stared in amazement. Seated in front of him, leaning towards him slightly with an expression of concern, was none other than the mysterious girl he had encountered at the shop on Saturday. There was nothing remarkable about her clothes; she was wearing faded jeans, a purple hoodie and trainers. Her hair was very striking; it hung like a sheet of pure gold, glistening as the light caught it. Her eyes were a piercing blue, and Jack had an uncanny feeling that she was looking right through him. But still her skin remained her most distinctive feature; it was almost transparent.

"Are you OK, Jack?"

"Yeah – I think so." His head was spinning. "Yeah – I'm fine. Thanks."

Then:

"But how – who – I mean – how do you know me? What are you doing here? Who are you, anyway?" The words tumbled out.

The girl smiled.

"I'm Celeste."

Celeste! What a ridiculous-sounding name. He was sure that there was no-one at school with that name.

"You're – you're not from St Michael's are you?"

"No." The girl smiled again, rather secretively.

"So – where are you from, then?"

"I don't live around here. Not most of the time, anyway." She had a far-away, dreamy expression on her face.

"Then how do you know me? How did you know my name?"

Another enigmatic smile.

"I've seen you around before. And I've heard quite a lot about you."

"Have you?"

"Oh, yes."

Jack wondered from whom, but something in the girl's demeanour defied him to ask. He tried another approach.

"What are you doing around here? I mean – I'm glad that you were around, you know. Thanks for helping me out. But – why?"

"Let's just say I've been looking out for you."

Was she winding him up? Jack eyed her suspiciously. The girl was looking straight at him, no hint of sarcasm on her face. Jack's eyes met hers, and once again he had the strange sensation that she was looking right into him. He shifted his gaze uncomfortably and stared at the ground.

It was Celeste who broke the silence.

"It's time for me to go." She stood up, brushed grass off her jeans, and stated in a matter-of-fact tone, "I'll see you later, Jack."

She touched him lightly on the shoulder, turned and walked away.

"Hang on a sec, Celeste – wait a minute!" Jack called after her. She did not respond, but kept walking, with the same graceful movements Jack had noticed on Saturday at the shop. It was no use shouting after her; she was resolute. He watched, fascinated, as she retreated into the distance, her stride purposeful, arms swinging slightly, head and shoulders erect. Jack watched until she disappeared from view. He continued to sit, motionless, his mind whirling.

What was going on? Who was this strange girl? All he knew was her name: Celeste. She had not told him where she came from. She seemed to know him, but had appeared reluctant to discuss it. What was she hiding? And what did she mean by saying she had been looking out for him? Why on earth should she care about *him*, Jack? Yet she had sounded serious, and had gone out of her way to rescue him from what could have been a very nasty situation.

Jack suddenly felt cold. Looking up into the fading light he realized the time. His mum would be wondering where he had got to. He sprang to his feet, and doubled over in pain. Gingerly, Jack straightened up and slowly made his way home.

3

A Midnight Escapade

Jack had quite a lot of explaining to do when he finally arrived home, dishevelled, sore and limping.

"Jack! What on earth happened to you?" was his mother's anxious greeting.

Jack had been so bemused by the whole encounter with Celeste that he had not thought about what he was going to tell his mum. He did not want to recount the incident with Harvey; he knew that she would not approve of his fighting, even if he had been defending someone who was being unfairly bullied. But he could not think of any alternative explanation as to why he was so late home and covered in cuts and bruises that was any more likely to appease her.

"Oh – nothing much," he said airily.

"Jack!" He hated it when she said his name in that 'I know you're not telling me the truth' tone of voice. "It doesn't look like nothing to me."

"It's no big deal, Mum. I just got into a bit of a – fight – that's all." There was little point in lying; Jack gave as few details as possible. It was not made any easier by his sister, Lucy, who sat there wide-eyed, interrupting frequently. He did not mention Celeste. He would not have known where to begin, and he did not want to admit to having been rescued by a girl!

Eventually, with both his mother's and sister's curiosity satisfied, Jack sat down to tea. He was ravenous. Lucy sat opposite him, a smug smile curling on her lips.

"What's your problem?" Jack muttered irritably.

"Where's your bag?" Lucy demanded. Then, in a louder, triumphant tone, "Mum, Jack's come home without his school bag!"

Jack wanted to slap the smile off her face, but thought that he was already in enough trouble. Besides, his mum would have noticed sooner or later. With everything that had happened he had completely forgotten about his bag. He must have left it in the lane, where he had dropped it on meeting Harvey and the other boys.

The evening found Jack trudging wearily back to the fateful lane to retrieve his bag. Fortunately, it was still there, although it had evidently been thrown in a puddle, and its contents strewn across the ground. No prizes for guessing who was responsible, Jack thought grimly. He salvaged his scattered belongings and flung them into the sodden bag. A grey exercise book lay opened and face down in the mud. Jack's heart sank; it was his science book. It looked as though the boys had been using it as a football; virtually every page was muddied and torn, and Jack realized in horror that the latest piece of homework had been completely removed. How was he going to explain that to Mr. Lucas? He had already received one detention over the ill-fated experiment. Things were going from bad to worse. One thing was certain: he would get even with Harvey Grahams if it was the last thing he did!

Jack's resolution strengthened over the next two days. He had to miss football practice in order to rewrite his homework, and endured a humiliating berating from Mr. Lucas in front of the whole class over the state of his book. The worst part was watching Harvey's smug face; he was obviously relishing every moment. Jack had informed his best friends, Alfie and Callum, of Monday's escapade, and they agreed that anyone picking on someone like Marcus Littlewood was nothing but a bully and a coward.

But although Jack felt enraged towards Harvey, he had a more pressing matter on his mind: Celeste. He could not stop thinking about his bizarre encounter with her, and the more he thought about it, the stranger it seemed. She had seemed very secretive about her identity, merely stating she was "looking out" for him. Was it just a fortunate coincidence that she had been there when Harvey and his sidekick were about to beat him senseless? Or had she been following him without his realizing it? Maybe she had followed him into the shop on Saturday as well? But why should she care? It just did not make sense.

Other things did not make sense either. Celeste must have been hiding in the hedge, positioned in such a way that he could hear her but the others could not. And then she had grabbed hold of him and somehow dragged him through the hedge, out of the lane and on to a bank some distance away, where Harvey was unlikely to catch up with him. How on earth had she been able to do that? Did she have superhuman strength? Jack could not remember how he had got from the front of the hedge to the bank – he must have blacked out. It had all happened so quickly that he had not had time to work out what was going on. But now, thinking back through the events, there were a lot of unanswered questions.

Then there was Celeste's unusual appearance. She was more than just striking; she looked almost unreal. Those piercing eyes and that sheet of gold hair. And that unearthly white skin. Maybe she was not really a girl at all. Perhaps she was a ghost! Jack knew his imagination was running wild; he did not even believe in ghosts. But something about her disturbed him, and he could not get her out of his mind.

"I'll see you around, Jack." Those had been her parting words. He wondered whether he would ever see her again.

One night about a week later, Jack could not sleep. He lay in bed, mulling over the past fortnight's events for about the fiftieth time. Outside, the air was still and strangely silent. Suddenly he heard a tapping on the window. At first Jack thought he must have imagined it, but as he lay there it grew more insistent. Curious, he padded over to the window and flung open the curtains.

Whatever he expected to find, it was certainly not the sight that greeted him. There, crouching on the window-sill, hand raised to knock again on the pane, was the figure of a young girl. Jack started in fright. What on earth was going on? The girl lifted her head to look at him.

It was Celeste.

"Hello, Jack. Are you going to let me in?" She spoke as though it were the most natural thing in the world for her to be sitting on his window-sill in the middle of the night! Speechless, Jack fumbled to open the window, and Celeste swung her legs and body through, landing gracefully and easily on the bedroom floor.

"You took your time." She smiled at Jack's incredulous face. "I thought you were never coming!"

Jack found his tongue.

"What are you doing here? How did you get up here?"

"I thought it was about time I paid you a visit."

"You don't half choose your moments! Have you not heard of ringing the doorbell, like a normal person?"

"Then I'd have woken your mum and sister up," was the matter-of-fact reply.

Jack was about to ask how she knew he lived with his mum and sister, but Celeste broke in.

"There's something I want to show you, Jack." This time there was a note of urgency in her voice. "Will you come with me?"

"Yeah, OK." Jack was hesitant. "Where are we going?"

"You'll see. But Jack—" Her face was deadly serious as she turned to him now. "You'll have to trust me."

Once again Jack found himself speechless, although his mind was bursting with questions. Celeste's air of mystery coupled with her complete assurance somehow made any comments unnecessary. He hurriedly pulled on a pair of jeans and sweatshirt over his pyjamas, and kicked on his trainers, wondering what it was that Celeste wanted to show him. She was back at the open window, climbing up on to the ledge.

"Celeste! What are you doing?" Jack was suddenly alarmed.

She looked at him calmly. "Ready to go?"

"Not out there! We can go downstairs – I've got my own key."

Celeste shook her head. "No, Jack. We need to go out this way."

Was she mad? How exactly did she propose they reach the ground? By climbing down the drainpipe?

Celeste seemed to sense his thoughts. "It's easy, we'll jump."

"We'll what?!"

"We'll jump, Jack." She looked at him intently, and Jack had the same feeling as before that she was looking right into him. He shifted uncomfortably.

"Jack, do you trust me?"

Jack hesitated. A strange sensation swept over him: this moment suddenly seemed incredibly important, as though more depended on his answer than a jump from the window. It was as though his whole life was about to take a new direction. There was so much he did not understand. He knew nothing about this girl, who she was, where she was taking him, and why she appeared to have chosen him. Yet...

"Yeah, OK." Jack took a deep breath. "I trust you."

Her face lit up with pleasure – no, *more* than pleasure, it seemed to Jack. She almost glowed with delight.

"Excellent! Come on then." She reached out her hand to help him through the window, and before he knew it Jack was standing beside her on the ledge. The ground seemed miles below; instinctively he pressed his body against the solid glass. Celeste gave his hand an encouraging squeeze.

"Ready?"

He felt far from ready, but it was too late to back out now.

"We'll jump on the count of three."

His heart was pounding uncontrollably. Celeste's voice sounded miles away.

"One... two... THREE."

He could not move. Every muscle in his body was rigid and his legs felt like lead. But something was happening outside his control. A pressure was building behind his back, like a warm gust of wind. A warm glow bathed his feet, spreading upwards, until his entire body was engulfed.

"Ready – jump!" Celeste called beside him.

Suddenly his feet felt amazingly light. Closing his eyes, Jack leapt into the air. The next moment he was soaring, boundlessly, a wonderfully exhilarating feeling. It lasted only a few seconds, however, before he was plummeting to the ground.

"It's OK." Celeste was by his side, grabbing his hand. "Just follow me." She glided downwards, and Jack slowed into a gentle descent. The ground was advancing. Celeste reached it first, landing with her characteristic poise. Jack followed, less gracefully, and hit the ground with a thud. He skidded to a halt, lost his balance, and landed sprawled on all fours. Celeste was laughing.

"Not bad for your first go, Jack."

Jack stood up shakily and looked up at his bedroom window in disbelief. Had they really jumped from there? How on earth had they managed it? Common sense told him he should be dead, but instead, all he had suffered was scraped hands and knees. He turned to Celeste excitedly.

"That was so cool! How did we do it?" He felt wonderful. Celeste merely smiled.

"Fancy some more? Come on, then." Before Jack had a chance to answer, she had taken his hand and was instructing him, "Just run with me, and when I tell you, jump again."

They were off, running across the lawn and into the street, gathering speed with every stride. Jack had never run so fast or so easily in his life.

"OK, ready? Now – jump!"

This time Jack felt no fear. He leapt into the air, and instead of landing a second or two later, he was propelled forwards and upwards. The warm glow crept back over him, until his whole body tingled. He clung to Celeste's hand as he reached forwards with his arms, kicking his legs out behind him.

"Wow! This is amazing! Celeste – we're flying!"

They were indeed flying. Jack had never experienced anything like it – the feeling of floating effortlessly, completely free. They were high above the rooftops, a network of lights outlining the streets below.

"You see that hill straight ahead?" Celeste asked a few minutes later. "That's where we're heading."

A dark shape loomed in the distance. As they approached it the hill became more clearly visible, until finally it was within reach.

"Ready to land, Jack? We'll aim for that flat bit of grass over there." Celeste pointed to a grassy verge just ahead. She grabbed his hand again and helped him steer towards it. Just as Jack thought they were about to crash headlong into it, his legs swung forward involuntarily, bringing him back up to an upright position.

"Lean forward and bend your knees," Celeste instructed. "We're about to land."

Jack did so, bracing himself for the landing. This time he felt marginally more in control of his body, although that did not prevent him from gripping hold of Celeste's hand. They had slowed right down and were now gliding towards the verge. "Any moment now," Jack thought, "any moment..." – and his feet hit solid ground. He lurched forward, managed to steady himself, and slowly pulled himself upright. He had done it! He had landed! He looked at Celeste, grinning broadly.

"Nice one, Jack," she smiled back approvingly.

Jack had never before experienced such an incredible feeling of exhilaration. He could not quite believe what had just happened – it defied all logic and reason – yet here he was, standing on the hill overlooking his town, when less than an hour before he had been lying in bed at home. Once again his mind buzzed with numerous questions. There was now no doubt that Celeste was no ordinary girl. Who else had he ever met who could fly?! She clearly had special powers of some kind. The question was, who or what was she? She was looking intently down at the town which spread below them. Jack cast his eyes in the same direction. He had climbed this hill countless times during the day and enjoyed the view of the whole town. It looked completely different by night. Usually he could locate his street, and sometimes even his house if it was a particularly clear day. Now every house was shrouded in darkness; only the roads were discernible by the pathways traced by the streetlights.

"So much darkness." Celeste spoke softly, more to herself than to him, it seemed. "There's so much darkness over this town." She turned to Jack with sorrowful eyes. "Can you see it, Jack?"

Jack was startled. Of course it was dark, he was about to retort; it was the middle of the night for goodness' sake. But somehow he had the feeling that Celeste was referring to something else, although he had no idea what. He looked again at the scene below, concentrating on the little beads of light that punctuated the pervading darkness. As his eyes adjusted to the night scene, Jack could make out the outlines of some of the more prominent buildings: the leather factory on the edge of town, the town hall in the centre, a church spire rising in the distance. His eyes lingered on the town hall; floodlit, it presided over all the other buildings, and was an impressive sight. But Jack noticed something else. In the corner of the building was what appeared to be a black spot, casting a shadow over it, and growing in intensity. It was not an isolated spot, Jack realized.

Small patches of darkness had emerged across the town, ugly and menacing. He shuddered.

"I can see spots – dark spots all over the place."

Celeste's face lit up.

"You can see them?" She sounded genuinely excited.

"Yeah – so what?" Jack was puzzled by her sudden change in demeanour.

"Jack." Her piercing blue eyes were fixed on him and her face was solemn. "This means your eyes have been opened. You're ready."

Eyes opened? Ready? Ready for what? Jack's mouth fell open and he stared at Celeste, speechless. What on earth was she talking about now? What had she said to him earlier in his bedroom? "There's something I want to show you." Was this what she had meant – a night view of the town covered in dark spots? Had she dragged him out of bed just for that? He found his voice.

"This is too weird. Celeste, you've got to tell me what's going on. Who are you? And what do you want with me?" There. He had finally asked the questions that had been plaguing him for the last two weeks.

Celeste took a deep breath.

"OK. I couldn't tell you before – it was too soon. But now I believe you are ready." She paused, frowned slightly, then continued. "I told you last time we met that I wasn't from around here. I didn't just mean that I'm not from this town; I'm from another world altogether."

So his earlier suspicion had been right; she was a ghost! Or was she perhaps an alien from another planet?

"You see, Jack, this world, this earth, isn't all it seems. You see people going about their business, day after day, as though that's all there is to life. And that is all that some people see. But beneath that there is a whole different world. It's made up of two kingdoms which are at war with each other: the Kingdom of Darkness and the Kingdom of Light."

"So which are you from?"

"Light."

"And where is this 'Kingdom of Light'?"

"It's everywhere. It's all around you, if you can only see it."

"And what about the other one – Darkness?"

"The same. It's all around. In fact, it's here. Those patches that you saw down below – they're all part of the Darkness." Her voice became even more solemn. "And it's growing. It's spreading in this town."

A chill crept down Jack's spine as she uttered those words.

"But I still don't understand." He was bewildered. "What's all this got to do with me?"

"You have been chosen, Jack, to join the Light side and to fight against the Darkness. That is what I have been sent to tell you."

Jack was dumbfounded. This was all growing stranger by the minute.

"What do you mean, you've been sent to tell me? Sent by whom?"

"By the Master. The Lord of Light."

"So – what does that make you?"

An enigmatic smile curled on Celeste's lips.

"I'm one of his messengers. Sent to bring a message especially for you. Some people like to think of me as an angel."

Now Jack was convinced his ears were deceiving him. Had she just called herself an angel? A ghost he could just about believe, perhaps even an alien – but an angel? That was preposterous!

"You don't look much like an angel to me," was all he could think of in response (as though he had ever seen one before!), realizing how foolish his words sounded.

"What did you expect – a white nightie and wings and a halo? There's a lot more to us angels than the pictures you see on the Christmas cards, you know." She did not sound offended, but rather amused.

Jack could not think of a suitable reply. He was struggling to make sense of her words.

"It's OK," Celeste spoke gently, "you don't have to decide now. You need some time to think about it." She touched his arm lightly. "Have another look down there."

He looked again at the town below. The patches of darkness were clearer now, distinct from the blanket of night that covered the town. And there was something that he had not noticed before: a few patches of light – brilliant, dazzling light – interspersed throughout the town. Darkness and Light. Two opposing kingdoms. Was that what he could see? His eye fell upon a low oblong building towards the west of town. It was obscured by a patch which seemed larger, darker and more sinister than the rest, and threatened to consume the entire building. Jack realized with a shock what he was looking at.

"That's my school! Hey, Celeste – that massive dark patch over there is on my school!"

Celeste nodded gravely, but said nothing. They stood in silence for a few minutes, contemplating the scene below. Finally, Celeste spoke.

"I reckon that's enough for one night. Ready to go home?"

It was more of a command than a question. Jack took the hand she offered him without protest, and soon they were soaring through the night air, leaving the hill and its view behind them, back home. It seemed no time at all before they reached Jack's house.

"Don't let go of my hand, whatever you do. This could be a tight landing," Celeste instructed.

They were hovering outside his bedroom window, which remained open slightly following their earlier departure. Celeste surged forward, perfectly in line with the window, flung it wide open and landed noiselessly on the bedroom floor. Jack followed, clinging to her hand for dear life. He narrowly missed the window pane and dived into his room, catching his foot on the ledge as he did so.

"Aaaargh!" He skidded across the carpet and landed in a heap beside his bed.

"Not such a smooth landing that time, Jack!" laughed Celeste, as she helped him up, and then, turning abruptly, she strode back towards the open window.

"Time I was going." She gave him one final piercing look. "Think about what you've seen and heard tonight, Jack. And remember – the choice is yours."

And with that, she was gone.

4

Jack Makes His Choice

"Jack! JACK! Time to get up!"

"Huh? Hmmmfh... hmmmm."

Jack was dimly aware of his mother's voice, but he was far too comfortable to move. He pulled the duvet more tightly around him and buried his face in his pillow.

"JACK! You'll be late for school!"

Blearily, Jack opened his eyes and forced himself into a sitting position. Memories of the night's adventure flooded into his mind. It must have been a dream – a weird, nonsensical dream. He swung his legs out from under his duvet and winced. His hands and knees were smarting. Jack examined them; they were fresh grazes, there was no doubt about it. They could only have occurred during the past few hours. He slowly stood up and moved towards the window. Flinging open the curtains he made another discovery: the window was slightly open. Jack frowned. He always closed his window at night.

There was only one explanation. The events of the previous night must have been real. A shiver crept down his spine.

As he went through the motions of washing and dressing, Jack recalled the details of his latest encounter with Celeste. He thought of little else throughout the day. At times he still thought that he must have dreamt it all; it seemed too extraordinary to be true. Yet the events were vivid in his mind: the flight, the contrasting darkness and light over the town, Celeste's face as she spoke to him.

"You have been chosen to join the Light side, to fight against the Darkness." What were these worlds, these 'kingdoms' she had spoken about? And why should he, Jack, who was just an ordinary twelve-year-old boy, have been chosen to fight on anyone's side? Should he feel excited or afraid? As for Celeste's revealed identity, he had no idea what to make of that. After all, it wasn't every day that someone announced they were an angel! Angels belonged in old religious paintings and Christmas cards, not in real life, and certainly not in his, Jack's life. But it seemed that one had walked right into his life whether he liked it or not. The question was, what was he going to do about it? "The choice is yours," had been Celeste's parting words. He could either accept her invitation to join this kingdom of Light, whatever it was, or reject it and pretend that none of this had ever happened.

Throughout the following week Jack tried to carry on as usual. He sat through his lessons, attended football practice, argued with his sister, and joked around with Callum and Alfie, much as he did every week. Yet somehow things were not the same. Ordinary life felt somewhat dull; even his Xbox had lost its usual appeal. One afternoon he returned to the hill, and once again looked down upon the town. It was a clear day and sunny, but it seemed covered by a grey mist, shrouding the town in a blanket of oppressiveness. A chill crept down his spine. There on the hall in the centre of the town was a dark shadow, just like the one he had seen during his nocturnal visit. He blinked hard and looked again; it was still there. Furthermore, it was spreading. Before his eyes, ugly dark patches appeared across the town, as though it had been struck by a plague. The chill crept from his spine into the pit of his stomach.

Out of nowhere a spot of light appeared, followed by another and another, until the whole town was dotted with spots of brilliant light. The contrast could not have been more marked.

Darkness and Light. Two opposing kingdoms? Jack's heart was beating faster now, with mingled trepidation and excitement.

Jack traced a row of low grey houses to locate his school. His heart missed a beat. The far right corner was completely black and cast a shadow over the entire building. There was something ominous about it. He stared, mesmerized.

Eventually Jack tore himself away and made his way slowly down the hill. He did not feel ready to go home just yet, and could not get rid of the image of the shadow over his school; it was horrible. Without really knowing why, he began walking back in that direction.

He did not reach the school, however. The town appeared to be back to normal as he walked through it; people were going about their usual business and Jack saw no more dark shadows or spots of light. Relief washed over him; perhaps he had imagined it after all. Or, more likely, it was the light and shadows cast by the setting sun. Yes, that was a more rational explanation.

Jack felt an inexplicable urge to turn down a narrow alleyway. It was not on his route, but he felt drawn like a magnet by some external force.

The alley was deserted, a stray cat skulking around the dustbins the only sign of life. Cautiously Jack made his way along the narrow path, trying not to trip over the cracked paving slabs. A sudden noise made him jump. The path was framed by a brick wall on either side, with only a few dustbins visible. There it was again: a low hissing which seemed to be coming from the brickwork. As Jack stared, perplexed, a shadow rose from behind a dustbin and, growing in intensity, crept up the wall until it loomed over the whole alleyway. At the same time an odour emanated from the site, a foul smell like rotting flesh. The hissing turned into a piercing shriek, and a violent movement overturned the dustbin with a clatter, its contents spewing on to the path. A dark shape emerged from the rubbish, darker even than the shadow behind. Jack could not make out any of its features except one: a pair of glinting green, menacing eyes. The creature leapt into the air, and with another scream, hurtled towards Jack. He pressed himself against the brick wall, not a moment too soon, as it steamed past, hissing and spitting. Jack caught a glimpse of a ferocious face with bared teeth, a serpent-like torso, four clawed feet and a black pointed tail, flailing furiously as it retreated up the alleyway and disappeared into the shadows. The stench as the beast screeched past was suffocating, and Jack clapped his hand to his mouth to prevent himself from vomiting.

He stood, motionless. What on earth was it? Jack had never seen anything like that in his life – it was like something out of a horror film.

Suddenly the place was flooded with light. A figure stood in the spot where the creature had vanished. Jack recognized her instantly.

"Celeste! Am I glad to see you!"

"I thought I might find you here." Celeste walked towards him.

"Did you see that – thing – that just went past? What on earth was it?"

"Yeah, I saw it," Celeste said calmly. "Although I didn't really need to – I could smell it a mile off!"

"What was it?" Jack asked again.

Celeste fixed him with one of her solemn gazes.

"You remember what I told you about the Dark and Light kingdoms? Well, that was a creature of the Darkness. Not a pretty sight, was it? Or smell!"

That was rather an understatement! The beast had looked terrifying, but Jack was not about to admit that. He searched for another question, trying to sound nonchalant.

"So, if it's come from this Darkness kingdom place that you keep going on about, what's it doing here?"

"Creatures like that – demons – are everywhere, Jack. You've passed them hundreds of times before, but you've never been aware of it. Remember what I told you: the Darkness is all around, whether you can see it or not. But—" Here she broke off with a dazzling smile. "So is the Light."

Jack perched on a dustbin in a vain attempt to steady his pounding heart and spinning head. He was trying to absorb Celeste's words, but the image of that ferocious beast, whose sulphuric stench still lingered in the alleyway, was overpowering. There was no denying its gruesome reality. He could no longer pretend that nothing was happening, and the need to respond was becoming increasingly clear. Celeste had presented him with a choice: to join the kingdom of Light and, in doing so, the fight against Darkness. He could accept or reject this invitation, but he had to decide which.

What if he was to reject it? He felt entitled to do so; after all, Celeste had walked into his life uninvited and unannounced, quite literally out of the blue. She had told him that the world he had always known was not at all as it seemed, and was proposing that he enter this world of hers that he had never heard of and was not entirely sure he believed in. He could just imagine his friends' reaction, or even his mother's for that matter. They would all think that he had gone mad! It was not too late to walk away; he could say goodbye to Celeste and in a few weeks would feel as though none of this had ever happened.

Or would he? His first encounter with her flashed into his mind: standing at the checkout, turning and winking at him, then vanishing as suddenly as she had appeared. That had been followed by her dramatic rescue of him in the middle of his fight with Harvey Grahams. As if that had not been bizarre enough, she had then turned up on his bedroom window-sill in the middle of the night and taken him flying across the town. Impossible. Crazy. Things he never would have believed. Yet they had happened and had happened to him, Jack. And now this creature, this demon of Darkness that he could not ignore…

He shuddered. If this was what Celeste's kingdom of Darkness was like he definitely did not want anything to do with it!

But what about the Light? Celeste had come from another world altogether, which brought him back to her original question: did he want to join this kingdom? He could refuse, but what if that meant turning down the biggest adventure of his life? A tingling excitement was creeping over him. There was so much that he did not know or understand, but something inside was telling him that he knew enough to make his decision. Suddenly, he recalled Celeste standing on his window ledge, and her words, "Do you trust me?" Only minutes later he had been soaring through the air, high above the rooftops, the most exhilarating moment of his life. What other unimaginable experiences lay ahead if he dared to trust her word again and become a part of her world?

"OK, I'll do it, Celeste. I'll join your side."

While Jack had been deliberating, Celeste had been resolutely pacing up and down the alley. She stopped mid-step and turned to Jack, beaming.

"I knew you would!"

"So what happens now?"

"Come with me and I'll show you."

Jack followed her across the cracked pavement, his heart still pounding. He had made his choice. Now the adventure had really begun.

5

Three Rusty Nails

They arrived at the meadows on the edge of the town. The late afternoon sun cast swathes of light across the ground. It was a welcome sight after the dark shadows of the alleyway. The putrid air still lingered in Jack's nostrils; he took a long, deep breath and immediately felt better. Standing in this tranquil place, with Celeste by his side and the demon far behind them, he felt ready to face anything. His excitement was mounting by the minute as he waited impatiently for Celeste's next revelation.

She appeared to be in no hurry to speak. She was surveying the scene, and Jack felt for a moment as though they were back on the hill overlooking the town. What was she looking at? Could she see something he could not? Celeste knelt silently on the grass, her head bowed. Feeling slightly uneasy, Jack watched her, pale and motionless as a marble statue. After what seemed an age she finally stood, with her characteristic poise, and turned to face him. She was wearing her most solemn expression.

"You have chosen the way of the Light. It is the right way, but I need to warn you that it is not an easy one. You have started out on a long and difficult journey, and you will face dangers along the way. Many before you have embarked on a similar journey and have given up because they found the path too hard. A few have kept going, right to the end. That demon you saw a little while ago, Jack, was just the beginning. There will be many more like that – some much worse. You'll need every bit of courage you've got. And they don't all look like that one, either – they're devious creatures, and come in all sorts of disguises. So you need to be cunning to outwit them."

Jack was starting to feel extremely uncomfortable. His earlier enthusiasm was fast evaporating, and suddenly he was not at all sure he wanted to continue. But Celeste had not finished. She flashed him one of her dazzling smiles.

"That's the bad news. The good news is that you're not on your own! I told you before that you have been chosen, and not by me – I'm only the messenger. You have been chosen by the Master himself. He will guide you through and show you the way to go."

"But I don't know who 'the Master' is. I've never met him – I've never even heard of him."

"You'll meet him soon enough. He's with you now – in fact, he always has been. It's just that you've never realized it. Your eyes weren't opened before."

She was talking in riddles again. It was infuriating. But before he could object, Celeste was continuing:

"You remember what I said that night on the hill? That Darkness and Light are at war with each other? Well, you've entered that war, Jack. You're part of it now. The Master has chosen you to fight on his side, and he has a job for you to do. The Darkness is closing in on this town and we need all the forces of Light to fight against it. Your school is the main target; you saw yourself how much Darkness is covering it. We need to win it back if we are going to win the battle for this town. And you've got an important part to play, Jack."

Jack was stunned. Who was he, to have been specially chosen to fight in the war of this supernatural world? Just an ordinary twelve-year-old schoolboy who could not even get into the football team. There was nothing special about him.

"But – why me? I'm nobody. Why not choose someone like Harry Richards – he's the captain of the school football team? Or Amy Smithson – she's really brainy."

"You might not think you are very important, Jack, but that's not how the Master sees you."

Jack eyed her suspiciously, but he could see that she was deadly serious. He took a deep breath.

"OK, then. Where do I start?" He was beginning to feel excited again at the prospect of taking part in something so much bigger than him and his (up until now) unremarkable life.

"You start from where you are," was Celeste's un-enlightening reply.

"But – how will I know what to do?"

"You'll work it out as you go along."

"But, you'll be with me, right? You'll show me the way?"

"I'll be there if you need me. But it's down to you now. You know enough for now."

"I don't know anything, Celeste!"

"You know enough for now," she repeated emphatically. "And the Master will show you the rest. But you need to be patient and wait. And trust."

Patience! Trust! That was easy for her to say! She wasn't the one who was about to go off and face all sorts of dangers for the sake of something or someone she knew next to nothing about.

As though reading his thoughts, Celeste reached out one hand and snatched at the air. From nowhere something appeared in her hand. She passed it to Jack.

"Here – take this. It will equip you for the battles ahead."

She placed a small leather drawstring bag in his hand. Jack went to open it, but Celeste placed a restraining hand on his arm.

"Not just yet. Wait a few minutes. Now, listen." Her voice was urgent but at the same time gentle. "I know you feel uncertain about all of this. You are not sure what to expect, or what is expected of you. You're not even sure if you totally believe it – it's all so new and strange and incredible. You're wondering how you can possibly take part in a war against anything, when you have no weapons to fight with and don't even know what will happen tomorrow. Don't worry. That is how it is supposed to be. You'll find the way, one step at a time."

She paused for a moment, as Jack digested this information. Then she continued.

"If you ever lose your way completely, come back here, where you started. You will find the help you need."

Jack cast his eye across the meadow, tracing the outline of the trees and trying to etch them into his memory. He turned back to Celeste, but she was gone.

"Celeste! Celeste!" He looked around in all directions, but there was no sign of her. She had vanished.

Jack suddenly felt very alone and more than a little afraid. He did not know when he would next see Celeste, if indeed he would ever see her again. He was clutching the little bag she had given him. He opened it with eager, trembling hands, hoping that it held something that would help him in this strange quest. Inside he could see a flash of metal. His spirits rose; perhaps it was a knife or a gun. Celeste had said that it would equip him for battle.

Jack pulled out a large rusty nail, followed by a second and a third. They were heavier than regular nails, and their razor-sharp points were tinged with a dull red substance. It was blood, Jack realized with a shock. He stared at them with morbid fascination. What had they been used for? Why had Celeste given them to him? And how on earth were they going to help him in his battle? Celeste had told him to be patient, to wait and to trust. It seemed that he was left with little choice than to comply. Baffled, Jack replaced the monstrous nails in the leather bag, stuffed it into his pocket, and slowly headed home.

6

The Shadow in the Corridor

When Jack arrived at school the following morning, everything seemed the same as usual. The playground was alive with noise, as groups of boys and girls loitered and chatted as they waited for the summons of the bell. Jack looked intently for the sinister shadow he had seen covering the school, but there was no sign of it. A sense of relief was mixed with confusion. Celeste's abrupt departure the previous afternoon had left him feeling somewhat abandoned and far from ready to confront whatever dark presence loomed ahead.

"Hi, Jack." A stocky boy with dark spiky hair appeared, grinning, at his side.

"All right, Alfie?"

"Done any revision for this history test?"

They had history first period, Jack's least favourite subject, largely because it was taught by the severe deputy head, Mrs. Grimshaw. He had completely forgotten about the test, and had not opened his books for weeks.

"Oh no – I'm dead!" he groaned. Deciding that he had better go inside and have a quick look through his work before registration, he headed towards the door with a hurried, "See you later, Alfie."

"Yeah, see you."

As he hurtled down the corridor and around a corner towards his classroom, he nearly collided with a Year Nine girl.

"Watch it!" she muttered, glaring at him.

"Sorry!"

Jack's last-minute revision did not pay off. An hour later he had failed the test and was bottom of the class and in Mrs. Grimshaw's bad books. Now she was informing the class about witch-hunting in the seventeenth century. Jack turned to Alfie, grinning.

"I reckon old Grimshaw's a witch. Shame we can't burn her at the stake!"

Unfortunately he spoke louder than he intended. Mrs. Grimshaw stopped mid-sentence and fixed Jack with an icy stare. Her bony shoulders were raised and her chin jutted forward, always a bad sign. A deadly silence fell. Jack could not help thinking how much she actually did resemble a witch, with her long black skirt, grey straggly hair and hooked nose. Her voice was cold and measured.

"Jack Fletcher, as you are clearly unable to do or say anything constructive today, perhaps you would like to leave the room and let the rest of the class get on with their work."

As Jack slung his bag over his shoulder and walked towards the door, she added ominously, "I'll see you at the end of the lesson."

Standing outside the classroom, the earlier feeling of loneliness returned. The history lesson had been boring, but this was even worse, and there was still over half an hour to wait until break time. Gazing down the deserted corridor, something caught his eye. It was a bright spot of light, hovering just below the ceiling. Jack began to walk towards it, half expecting Celeste to appear at any moment. The light appeared to be moving; when Jack reached the place he had first seen it, he saw it further along the corridor. It remained tantalizingly out of reach, and Jack continued to follow it, until it finally rested over a white door. It was the entrance to the girls' toilets. He could hardly go in there! Jack stood rooted to the spot, unsure what to do next, and feeling rather foolish. A minute later the door swung open and out stepped a fair-haired girl wearing glasses. Jack recognized her as the girl he had nearly walked into earlier that morning. Embarrassed, he wanted to turn away, but could not take his eyes off the beam of light, which was now hovering above the girl's head. She was staring at him too, not in annoyance, but with a kind of fascination. She was the first to speak.

"This might sound a funny question, but do you by any chance belong to the Light?"

Jack was taken aback, and for a moment did not know how to respond. He answered hesitantly, "Yeah, kind of."

The girl frowned.

"Well, either you do or you don't."

"No – I mean yes – I do. It's all a bit new to me, though. I haven't really got used to the idea yet. Why, do you?"

"Yes, I do. And I've been looking for ages for someone else at school that belongs too. You're the first person I've met here." She was grinning from ear to ear. "I'm Alison."

"Jack."

"It's really great to meet you," she enthused. "I've been a bit lonely on my own. My friends don't really understand about the Light. They think I've lost the plot a bit." This last sentence was uttered with a rueful smile.

"You've told your mates, then?"

"Yeah, of course. Haven't you?"

"No, not yet." He could not imagine how he would even begin to explain to Alfie and Callum the events of the past few weeks.

As they stood talking, Jack became aware that the corridor had darkened, as though a storm were brewing. He glanced out of the window; it was bright and sunny outside. Looking ahead, he noticed that a shadow had fallen across the back wall. He shuddered and turned to Alison. She had seen it too and was staring at it, wide-eyed and open-mouthed.

"The Darkness," she murmured. "You know about the Darkness, Jack?"

Jack nodded. The shadow was creeping towards them, intensifying by the second.

"What should we do?"

"Follow it."

"Are you sure?"

"Yes. Come on, Jack."

Alison stepped forward resolutely, and Jack followed uncertainly. He could remember only too well the last time he had encountered such a shadow, and was in no hurry to repeat the experience. He wished desperately that Celeste was with them; she would know what to do.

Silent and stealthy, the shadow slid along the length of the corridor, turned a corner, and continued up a flight of stairs, darkening one step at a time. Jack and Alison followed cautiously. Neither spoke until they reached another corner.

"It's heading for the library," Alison whispered.

She was right. The shadow bent sharply left and stopped right outside the library door. It drew itself to a great height, covering the surrounding area in total darkness, then shrank down and disappeared under the doorway. The pair looked at one another in amazement.

"Shall we go in?"

"I dunno." Jack did not want to appear cowardly in front of Alison, but the memory of the demon in the alleyway was at the forefront of his mind. However, his curiosity won, so he added quickly, "Yeah, come on, then."

He opened the door tentatively and stepped inside, Alison right behind. All was quiet. A few older students were seated at the tables, their heads buried in books. Jack scanned the shelves; there was no sign of the shadow.

"Where's it gone?" he muttered.

"Maybe it's down the other end," Alison suggested. "Let's have a look."

"Shhhh!" A harassed-looking girl peered irritably from her book.

Jack and Alison crept around the library, looking behind every shelf and in all the corners. The shadow was nowhere to be seen. They exchanged puzzled glances.

"I don't understand," said Alison. "Where on earth can it have gone?"

Jack shrugged. "Search me."

"Will you two either shut up or go out! Some of us are trying to work in here!" It was the irritable girl again. Alison rolled her eyes.

"Come on, we might as well go."

Outside the library they were able to speak undisturbed.

"What do we do now?" Jack wondered.

Alison was silent for a minute, before saying thoughtfully, "I reckon we should go back when there's no-one else about."

"You do?"

"Yeah. I think that thing's hiding in there, and won't come out again until it's quieter."

"But we saw it in the corridor earlier. It wasn't hiding then."

"No, but we were the only people around. No-one else would have seen it."

There was an uncomfortable pause. Then Jack said slowly, "Do you think it wanted us to see it?"

Alison looked fearful. "I don't know."

They were silent again. Jack's heart was beating fast. They had started something and could not stop it now, even if they wanted to. Alison was right; they had to go back.

"We'll go back after school," he said decisively. "It'll be empty then."

"What about the Old Bat?"

The 'Old Bat' was an unflattering reference to Miss Batstone the school librarian. She was more affectionately known by both staff and students as 'Old Batty' due to her eccentric mannerisms. She was usually seen with her nose in a book. But woe betide any unfortunate student who was late in returning their books or, worse still, had damaged or misplaced those sacred objects. The mild, absent-minded Miss Batstone had another side to her which had earned her the irreverent nickname 'Old Bat'.

"She'll be gone by then," Jack said confidently. "I'll meet you here outside the library just after the bell. That's if I'm still alive by then!" He suddenly remembered that Mrs. Grimshaw had not yet finished with him. "I'll tell you about it later," he added, seeing Alison's bewildered expression. "I'd better get going."

"OK. See you back here after school."

"Yeah, see you."

Jack reluctantly retraced his steps to the history room to face the wrath of the dreaded Mrs. Grimshaw. However, this was nothing compared to his apprehension about confronting the ominous shadow and whatever lay behind it.

The afternoon bell rang all too soon. Usually Jack could not wait for the school day to end, especially a day like this, following the lecture he had received from Mrs. Grimshaw, culminating in yet another detention. It was only a couple of weeks since his last one! But today the hours passed alarmingly quickly, and before he knew it Jack was climbing the stairs which led to the library, wishing that his detention was taking place now and not on Monday.

Alison was already there, waiting for him.

"You took your time!"

"The bell only went five minutes ago! And I was right over in the science labs."

"Oh." She bit her lip nervously. "It felt longer than that."

"Well, I'm here now so shall we go in?" Jack tried to sound casual, but he was acutely aware of the tension in his voice.

He pushed open the door before he had time to think about it, and froze. He could hear a movement behind one of the bookshelves. Alison crept forward for a closer look. A moment later she had darted back and was mouthing at Jack, "The Old Bat!"

It was too late to retreat without being noticed. Jack motioned towards the end of the nearest bookshelf, and they crouched behind it. The only sound was Miss Batstone shuffling up and down along the shelves, straightening her books as she went. Every now and again she let out a sigh, as though lamenting the state they had been left in by careless students. She was taking forever; was she reading them too? The shuffling grew closer; peering out, he saw Miss Batstone's plump legs just a few metres away. Motioning to Alison he crawled around the other side of the shelf, and the pair crept along it, hardly daring to breathe. Miss Batstone continued at the same unhurried pace; she did not appear to have seen them. Reaching the opposite end, Jack peered around again. She was at a safe distance now, her dumpy frame bending down to the lowest shelf. He gestured towards the next row of shelves, which had already been scrutinized, and dived behind it, Alison at his heels. Jack's foot hit the corner of the shelf with a thud as he shot around. The pair froze, Alison glaring at him.

"Timothy! Is that you?" Miss Batstone peered short-sightedly over her glasses.

Timothy was Mr. Collins the caretaker's cat, and a frequent visitor to the school premises. Seeing no sign of the ginger tom, Miss Batstone returned to her books. Eventually, the last shelves were tidied and she was making her way to the door. She cast one final glance around the room, and seeing nothing amiss, shuffled away, a fat book clutched tightly under one arm.

"Timothy! Is that you?" Alison mimicked, and they both burst out laughing. They had been so engrossed in hiding from Miss Batstone that they had almost forgotten their reason for coming.

Not for long, however. A deathly silence fell, and Jack could have sworn that the room darkened. He stood up slowly and cautiously looked around. All he could see were the rows of shelves that lined the library, every book positioned correctly in its place. Beside him Alison screwed up her nose.

"Jack, can you smell something?"

There was a faint but strangely familiar odour in the air. As they stood there it grew stronger and more pungent.

"It's disgusting!" Alison grimaced. "What on earth is it?"

Jack's heart missed a beat. It was unmistakable. He had only smelt it once before, but he would recognize that stench anywhere. The image of the black beast with its green eyes and bared teeth flooded into his mind and he shuddered.

Alison noticed, and asked with a look of concern, "Are you OK, Jack? You've gone really pale."

He did not, *could not*, answer. The smell was intensifying by the second and was almost suffocating. Alison gagged.

"I think I'm going to be sick! I need to get out of here." She started towards the door, and stopped in her tracks. A dark shadow loomed before them, without shape or form. From somewhere within it came a low hissing sound. They stood, transfixed, as the hissing grew louder. There seemed to be something behind the shadow, writhing and spluttering, trying to break out. They watched it take shape before their eyes: a narrow head with protruding ears, a long body out of which grew two gangly arms and a pair of bent legs. As the legs slowly straightened, the creature drew itself up to its full height and towered above them, a giant of a beast. Its features were becoming clearer now: a pair of clawed hands and feet, each the size of a football, and a thin, pointed face that looked as if it had been chiselled out of stone. Two vivid green eyes glared down, the only colour to pierce through the shadow.

Jack and Alison stood, petrified. The creature was staring at them, its thin lips stretching into a sinister smile. Then, before they knew what was happening, the gangly arms were reaching towards them, giant claws outstretched. Alison screamed, and Jack looked around wildly for a means of escape. The beast was blocking their direct access to the door; the only other possibility was to edge around the bookshelves and creep out that way. Grabbing Alison by the arm and yanking her sideways, Jack ran along the nearest row of shelves, away from the fearsome creature. He pressed his back against the wall and began stealing along it, pulling Alison along as he went. As they neared the door, Jack shot a look across the room. The coast was clear; the exit was only a few metres away. He ran towards it breathlessly. In less than a minute he and Alison would be safely on the other side, the demon behind them. He reached for the door handle and pulled it eagerly. As he did so he heard a piercing scream. The creature had appeared from nowhere, gripped hold of Alison's arm and was pulling her towards its lean body. A pointed tongue emerged to lick the thin lips, and green slime dribbled down the angular chin. Jack turned cold. Was it going to eat her? There was no time to think; he had to act. He dived forward and grasped Alison's ankle. He could feel the force pulling her away, and he tugged at her ankle in an effort to keep her from sliding further into the clutches of this evil beast. He was fighting a losing battle, however, and was being dragged along the floor. He saw a table just ahead, and wrapped one foot around the leg to anchor himself. For a moment he seemed to hold Alison still, and he clung on with all his might. The pressure pulling her back was unbelievably strong. He could feel his foot slipping, and fought desperately to keep it in place. Now the whole table was beginning to shift; he was not going to be able to hold his grip much longer. He twisted his head around to look up; to his horror, the long arms were coiling themselves around Alison's neck. In the next instant his foot was wrenched away from the table, and he was being dragged across the floor once again by an even greater force than before.

"Jack! Do something! It's choking me!" Alison was gasping for breath and could hardly get the words out.

What could he do? He was completely overpowered by this hideous creature yet he could not, *he must not*, give in.

Suddenly, he was aware of something in his blazer pocket pressing against his thigh. It was digging in, almost burning into his flesh. And then Jack remembered; it was the mysterious package that Celeste had given him only the day before. He had shoved it in his pocket and forgotten all about it. Her words came back to him in a flash: "It will equip you for the battles you are about to face." With one hand still desperately clutching hold of Alison's ankle, he thrust the other one into his pocket and pulled out the leather bag. Could it really help them? There was only one way to find out. He released his grip on Alison and with trembling fingers opened the bag and emptied its contents into his hand.

A scream filled the air. The creature had lifted Alison to its bony shoulders, its mouth gaping into a monstrous grin. Its arms were wrapped even more tightly around her neck. The nails were in Jack's hand. He had no idea what he was supposed to do with them, or how they could possibly fend off the beast, but there was no time to lose. Raising his arm, Jack aimed at the creature's chest and flung the nails with all his might.

And then something remarkable happened. The nails, appearing to take on a life of their own, flew like arrows towards the beast's heart and struck with perfect accuracy, a trail of light blazing behind them. It all happened in an instant: the beast let out a screech of terror, releasing the petrified Alison who dropped, limp as a ragdoll, on to the floor. An explosion of light filled the room, so blinding that Jack was forced to bury his face in his knees.

He did not know how long he remained in that position, arms wrapped tightly around his knees, head bent, eyes screwed shut. It could have been minutes, hours, he had no idea. He heard a hideous wailing which made his blood run cold, that he thought would never end. It gradually subsided until it finally disappeared altogether. But still Jack sat there, rigid, not daring to open his eyes. The only sound he could hear now was the pounding of his own heart.

Finally, he was roused by a movement beside him. Jack opened his eyes and slowly raised his head. Alison, who had been lying motionless on the floor since the beast relinquished her, had sat up and was looking around her, dazed and bewildered.

"Are you OK?" Jack asked shakily, noticing how pale she looked.

Alison nodded slowly. When she spoke it was in a whisper, but her breathing had returned to normal.

"What happened, Jack? Where's that – thing? Has it gone?"

Silently they surveyed the room. The bookshelves stood perfectly in order. The tables and chairs, similarly, were all positioned correctly, except one table, which had been pulled out of line. The library was quiet and strangely peaceful. There was no sign of the beast anywhere; it had vanished. All that remained was a faint, lingering odour.

Alison stood up slowly, and in doing so her foot hit something hard. She looked down and saw a flash of metal on the floor. Three long nails lay by her feet.

"What are they, Jack?"

"I'll tell you later – let's get out of here."

He bent down and scooped them into the palm of his hand. "Ow!"

They were scorching hot. Jack pulled the little bag from his pocket and gingerly replaced the nails. Then, without a word, he and Alison headed for the door.

7

More About the Master

The pair did not speak until they were safely out of the school gates. Fortunately, they had managed to elude both Mr. Collins and his infamous cat, and had sneaked out of the side entrance before it was locked. Outside, it was drizzling slightly, and the damp coolness was a welcome relief after the heat and stench of the library.

Jack turned to Alison, who was still very pale.

"Are you OK?"

She nodded, and it was a minute or two before she found her voice.

"What happened, Jack? What was that... monster?"

"You haven't seen anything like that before?"

"No, never. Why?" Alison was wide-eyed with astonishment. "Have you?"

"Just once before. Yesterday, actually." It seemed weeks ago.

"What – at school?"

"No, somewhere in town. Some side alleyway somewhere. But it wasn't as bad as this. It just went past me, didn't try to – you know – get me."

"I thought it was going to kill me. It was choking me. I really thought I was going to die."

Jack did not know what to say. He touched Alison's arm awkwardly.

"But you're OK now?"

"Yeah – just about."

They stood in silence for a minute, both struggling to make sense of their ordeal. Finally Alison spoke, slowly and thoughtfully.

"That thing was from the Dark kingdom, wasn't it?"

Jack nodded.

"Wow! My gran told me about creatures like that – demons, she called them. But I never thought they were actually real. To be honest, I thought she'd completely lost the plot."

"Did your gran see them, then?" Jack asked, interested.

"I don't know. I think she must have done – she seemed to know a lot about them. She knows a lot about everything, does Gran. It was her that told me about the Master and the Light, fighting against the Enemy and the Darkness. I didn't take too much notice of it all at first. It sounded pretty far-fetched to be honest, and – well – nothing to do with me and my life. But then things changed—" Alison broke off, a dreamy expression on her face.

Jack's interest was growing.

"What changed?" he asked eagerly. "What happened?"

Alison looked him straight in the face, her blue eyes searching his, as though deliberating whether or not she could trust him with what she was about to share. He met her gaze openly, eyes unblinking, silently pleading with her to talk to him. He had to know what was going on here, what this was all about, and it seemed that perhaps she was the one person who could tell him. She smiled, as though she had understood his unspoken communication, and opened her mouth to speak.

"I met the Master."

Jack's jaw dropped. Alison had met the Master! The Master that Celeste had spoken about, and assured him that he would meet soon. The Master who was engaged in war against these diabolical creatures of the Darkness, and who had flying messengers of Light on his side.

"How did you meet him? What's he like?" The questions tumbled out as Jack tried to absorb yet another unexpected piece of information.

Alison took a deep breath.

"It happened just over a year ago. I was going through a bit of a bad time – my mum and dad were splitting up, you know."

Jack nodded. "Yeah, I do know."

"Well, anyway, I went over to my gran's quite a lot while all that was going on, and we'd talk for hours about loads of things. She'd told me a bit about the Master before but, like I said, I hadn't taken much notice. But now it was like she was talking about a real person. She said he was always there with her, even though she couldn't actually see him, and that he'd always helped her through the really tough times – like when she fell down the stairs and broke her hip, and ended up having to go into a nursing home. I could tell by the way she talked about him that he was someone really important to her. She told me that he was there for me too – that he understood what I was going through and wanted to help me – I just had to ask him. I didn't understand what she meant at first, but she explained that the Master is there for everyone, but he doesn't force himself on anyone. It's up to each of us to choose whether or not we want to know him or not."

She paused here, looking wistfully into space.

"Yeah, so what happened next?" Jack tried not to sound impatient.

"One evening things were really bad at home. My dad was shouting, my mum was crying, my sister was screaming at them both to sort themselves out. I went and shut myself in my room – I'd really had enough. I pulled my duvet right over me, and I still couldn't drown them out. I felt like shouting and screaming as well. Then, while I was lying there, I said out loud, 'If you're really there, Master, please come and help me. I really need you.'"

"Then what happened?"

"Nothing at first. I just lay there. But then – I don't know how to explain it – it was really weird. It was like this warm feeling came over me, starting in my stomach, and then all over me. I was shaking – but it wasn't scary; it was nice. Sort of peaceful. And I just knew that I wasn't on my own and that things would be all right."

"And that was it?"

"Yeah, I guess."

"So you didn't actually see anyone or hear anyone?"

"No."

"So how do you know it was the Master? Couldn't you just have imagined it, just to make yourself feel better?"

Alison shook her head.

"No. No way. It was real. I know it was real. He was there with me. I could feel it."

"How?"

"I can't explain it, but I just know that he was there. That he's still here."

Alison looked into Jack's puzzled eyes.

"I know it's really hard to understand when you haven't experienced it yourself. I used to think Gran was off her trolley. It sounds like having an imaginary friend or something. But—" She broke off for a moment, then continued, "You saw that – thing – demon – whatever it was. That was pretty real."

Jack nodded slowly. "Yeah."

They remained in silence for a few minutes, both deep in thought. Then Alison spoke, suddenly remembering something.

"What were those nails that you picked up from the floor after that thing disappeared?"

Now it was Jack's turn to consider whether he could trust Alison. He was not good at talking to girls at the best of times, and he had never spoken to her before that morning. He did not really know anything about her, and neither did she about him. Yet they seemed to have something in common, and had just been through a terrifying ordeal together. And she had trusted him enough to talk about her encounter with the Master. Perhaps she would believe the things that had happened to him too.

Jack recounted the past fortnight's events, from his first glimpse of Celeste at the local shop, to his last meeting with her the day before, and her parting gift to him. Alison listened intently.

"Wow!" she breathed, when he had finished. "That's amazing! A real live angel! Gran told me about them – she called them 'messengers of Light' too – but I've never seen one. And she took you flying and everything? How cool is that!"

Jack was profoundly relieved. Not only did Alison believe his tale, but she seemed genuinely impressed and excited by it. He began to feel quite important at having received a visitation from an angel. It was clearly not an experience of which everyone could boast, even those who knew about the two warring kingdoms.

But that shed no further light on the mysterious nails. Jack retrieved them from his pocket and turned them thoughtfully in his hand. They had cooled by now, although they remained heavy. Alison peered at them, a look of repugnance on her face.

"They're lethal-looking things!" she exclaimed. "Look how long they are! And what's that on them – is it blood?"

"Yeah, I think so."

"From that – thing?"

"I dunno," Jack said thoughtfully, trying to remember how they had looked when Celeste first presented them to him. "I think there was blood on them already."

"Really?" Alison did not know whether she was repulsed or fascinated. "Let's have another look."

She grabbed the nails eagerly and stood staring at them, perplexed.

"What was it Celeste said about them?" she enquired.

"That they'd equip me for the battles I was about to face," Jack answered, surprised at how easily he recalled her words.

"And that's all she said? She didn't say where they came from or anything?"

"No. That was it."

It seemed to really bother Alison, and she continued to stand there, gazing at the treacherous-looking nails and frowning.

Jack was beginning to feel restless. And hungry. He had completely lost track of the time, but now that they appeared to be out of danger, at least at present, he realized with a shock that it was six o'clock, and teatime.

"I've got to go," he said abruptly. "My mum'll be wondering where I've got to."

"So will mine!" Alison exclaimed anxiously. Then, biting her lip, "So, what happens now?"

Jack shrugged his shoulders. "Search me." He produced his leather pouch and held out his hand for the nails. Alison returned them one by one, still transfixed. Jack carefully replaced them and thrust them deep into his pocket. He had no idea how or why, but knew now that somehow these rusty blood-stained nails had great power and had saved their lives. He would keep them on his person at all times from now on.

"Well, I guess I'll see you at school tomorrow?" Alison ventured hopefully.

"Yeah. See you."

They exchanged a brief, shy smile and went their separate ways to face the questions of their anxious parents.

8

Lucien's Plan

It was not until lunchtime the following day that Jack saw Alison again. He was sitting in the canteen with Alfie and Callum when she came rushing up to him, slightly red in the face.

"Hi, Jack, I've been looking for you everywhere." Alfie and Callum smirked at each other and moved their chairs noisily to make room for Alison. She sat down opposite Jack.

"I've been thinking about those nails," she murmured, leaning towards him, "and I think I know where they've come from."

"What!" spluttered Jack, almost choking on his mouthful of chips. He glanced sideways at his friends, but they were engaged in a belching competition and were paying them little attention.

"I couldn't stop thinking about it after I got home last night," Alison continued. "And then it came to me – it's all to do with the Master."

"How?" Jack was intrigued.

"You don't know much about him do you?"

"No." Jack felt slightly embarrassed. "Only what you and Celeste have told me, so not a lot."

"Well, a long, long time ago – about two thousand years ago, I think, back in the Roman times – the Master lived in our world. He was a human being, like us, but he had been sent from the kingdom of Light, and had special powers and could do amazing things."

"What sort of things?"

"Oh, loads of stuff. He cured people that were ill – people who were blind, or couldn't walk, or had horrible diseases – he made them better. He even brought one bloke back to life after he'd died."

"That's impossible!"

"Not for the Master. Anyway, he had lots of friends, and people who followed him, but he had lots of enemies too – people who were jealous of him, I think, and didn't like the things he was saying and doing. So they killed him."

"Oh." Jack felt deflated. What was the point of following a dead man who had lived two thousand years ago?

Alison seemed to guess his thoughts.

"But he came back to life again. He's still alive now – that's how I've met him, and my gran, and millions of other people. That's the amazing thing."

Jack was speechless. Alison continued, "But going back to the nails. That's what they used to kill him. They hammered long, spiky nails through his hands and feet, and nailed him to a tree. That's how they used to execute people in those days."

Jack shuddered. "That's gross!"

"Yeah, it is. It must have been a horrible way to die."

"And you're saying the nails Celeste gave me are the same ones that were used to kill the Master?"

"Yeah. Think about it." Now Alison sounded excited. "You threw the nails at the demon, and they knocked it down. It was absolutely terrified of them. There must have been something special about them for that to happen. There was nothing we could do – it would have killed me, and probably you as well. Some other power was protecting us, and it must have been the power of the Light. You remember there was a big blinding light when it happened? And it must have come from the nails. They belong to the Master and the Light, I'm sure of it."

Jack nodded slowly. He had to admit that Alison's explanation did make sense – as far as anything made sense anymore. He involuntarily patted the pouch in his pocket. The nails were far more precious than he had realized.

"You realize this isn't the end of it, Alison? The nails might have got rid of that demon, but there'll be others – they'll come back. I don't know what they want with us, but we've got ourselves mixed up in something big, whether we like it or not."

"You're right, Jack, but you're forgetting something. We've got the Light on our side."

Jack was suddenly aware that someone was watching them. A tall boy sat alone on the table opposite, chin cupped in his hands, elbows resting on the table. He had a narrow face, bony shoulders and sharp features. As Jack met his attentive gaze, his eyes darted away and he relaxed his posture. Had he been listening to their entire conversation? Jack did not recognize him, but guessed that he was probably in Year Ten or Eleven. The boy stood up and strode towards the door, a swagger in his gait.

"Do you know that boy over there? The tall one by the door?" Jack asked Alison.

"No. Never seen him before. Why?"

"Oh, it's probably nothing. I think he was listening to us, and just wondered if you knew him, that's all."

By now the canteen was emptying. Alfie and Callum had got bored of waiting for Jack and had wandered off. Jack and Alison sat quietly for a few minutes longer. There seemed to be little more to say, since neither of them knew what to do next. The bell sounded for afternoon lessons.

"We need to stick together, Jack. See you," were Alison's parting words, as she slung her bag over her shoulder and headed towards the door.

Not for the first time, Jack's head was spinning as he trudged off.

He spent the next few days warily looking out for shadows or spots of light around every corner, down every corridor and in every room that he entered, but he saw nothing. He even returned to the library, through necessity rather than choice, and saw no sign of anything untoward. However, it was difficult to relax, and his friends noticed that he was unusually tense.

"What's up with you, Jack?" Callum asked. "Has your girlfriend dumped you?"

"Ha ha, very funny," Jack retorted testily. "There's nothing up – I'm all right. And she's not my girlfriend."

"Yeah, whatever."

Then something happened to take his mind off everything for a while. Mr. Cartwright the sports teacher announced he was holding football trials the following week, one final opportunity to be selected for the school team. Jack signed up immediately. He had longed to join the team ever since he had started Year Seven, but in every trial had narrowly missed selection. Maybe this time would be different, he thought hopefully, as he scanned the list on the noticeboard to see who else had put their name down. His heart sank at seeing Harvey Grahams' name written at the bottom in its owner's square handwriting. Jack still felt considerable animosity towards him, in addition to which Harvey too had narrowly missed selection on a number of occasions, and was a formidable rival.

The trials were to be held on Tuesday lunchtime. On Monday Alison ran up to Jack at the school gate.

"Are you free after school today? I need to talk to you," she said breathlessly.

"I'm in detention."

"Oh. What about tomorrow lunchtime?"

"I've got football trials. Sorry."

"But Jack, this is really important. I've found out something that I need to talk to you about."

"Well, so is football important," Jack shot back. "It'll have to wait."

He walked off, leaving Alison standing at the gate, crestfallen.

At the end of the afternoon, as light-hearted boys and girls poured out of the school building and headed home, Jack trudged wearily to the detention room. Miss Batstone was on duty today, and smiled brightly as he walked in.

"What's your name, dear?"

"Jack Fletcher."

"Fletcher... Fletcher..." She peered short-sightedly at the list of names in front of her. "Oh yes – J. Fletcher – very good. Would you like to sit at the back, dear?"

"Lucien Ferndale," a voice behind Jack announced, and someone followed him to the back of the classroom. It was not until he was seated at the table beside him that Jack recognized him as the tall boy who had been watching him in the canteen. To Jack's surprise, he turned and winked at him. A few minutes later a note landed on Jack's desk. Seeing that the Old Bat had her nose buried in a book, he opened it and read a short message.

"Do you want to get your own back on Harvey Grahams tomorrow? Meet me outside afterwards. L.F."

Jack was stunned. How on earth did this boy know about his run-in with Harvey? And furthermore, why should it concern him? Only four people had been involved in the incident; he himself had only told Alison, Alfie and Callum about it, and he was sure it had gone no further. He had no idea what Harvey or his sidekick had been saying, although he would not have thought it was something they wanted to brag about. In any case, this boy Lucien could hardly be a friend of theirs if he was suggesting revenge. That left Marcus Littlewood. He had been grateful for Jack's rescue (rather too much, as far as Jack was concerned); perhaps he had informed this boy. Jack took a sidelong look at him. He could not imagine him associating with Marcus. Lucien looked cool and confident, in complete opposite to poor geeky Marcus.

Whoever this Lucien was, and however he knew about the incident with Harvey, Jack was eager to hear what he had to say. The events with Celeste, Alison and the demons had pushed his hostility to the back of his mind, but now all the anger resurfaced, along with a desire for revenge.

The hour's detention seemed the longest yet, and Jack felt that it would never end. The Old Bat appeared intent on finishing her book before releasing them. Finally, *finally*, the last page was turned and the book closed, and Miss Batstone looked up, beaming.

"Time's up. You may go now."

Lucien rose swiftly and sauntered out, Jack following at a short distance. He waited until they were outside and safely out of earshot before quickening his pace to reach Lucien. The tall boy turned towards him, a sly smile on his lips.

"So, you're interested in my idea?"

Jack nodded dumbly. Something in Lucien's tone defied him to ask any questions at this stage.

"You want to get even with Harvey Grahams?"

Jack nodded again, more vigorously this time. Lucien smiled.

"I don't blame you. And I can help you do it. You've got the football trial tomorrow, right? You and Grahams have both entered, and both want to get picked for the team? I think I could arrange it so that Grahams is taught a lesson and you make it into the team."

Jack found his voice. "How?"

"I'll be playing too. We'll tackle Grahams together; I'll bring him down, leaving the ball clear for you. With any luck you'll be able to score and win the game – and definitely win your place in the team. What do you say?"

Jack thought for a moment. It sounded simple enough, but would it work?

"How will I know when to tackle Harvey?"

"I'll give you the nod. You'll know, don't worry."

"Why would you want to do this?" Jack asked, a hint of suspicion in his mind.

Lucien shrugged his bony shoulders and smiled again, a sly, secret smile.

"Maybe I've got a score to settle with Grahams myself. Maybe I want to see the best man win. Maybe I just want to help you out of the goodness of my heart. Either way, my reasons don't concern you. What matters to you is that you beat Grahams, good and proper, and win your place in the team."

Jack could not argue with that. There was something slightly odd about Lucien's demeanour, but he seemed to want to help him, and it was worth a try.

"All right then, yeah. We'll do it. And – thanks."

"Don't mention it. Remember, wait for my nod."

"Yeah. Right."

"I'll see you tomorrow then."

And with that Lucien strode off, hands thrust into his pockets, whistling. Jack stared after him. There was some uncertainty in his mind, but by now he was growing accustomed to strange encounters with strange people. Perhaps his luck was finally about to turn. With this hopeful thought in mind, he sprinted all the way home and spent the evening cleaning his football boots in preparation for tomorrow's game.

9

Lucien Unmasked

Tuesday dawned, bright and sunny. Jack bounced out of bed and hurried to get ready for school. His football kit was clean and ironed and his boots were spotless. He sat down to breakfast with mingled excitement and apprehension, forcing himself to eat something. For once, even his sister seemed to be rooting for him.

"Good luck, Jack," she called out, as they parted at the school gate.

The morning lessons passed surprisingly quickly, although Jack could scarcely concentrate. In no time at all, the bell had rung for lunch and he rushed off to get changed. He felt a growing sense of unease as he made his way to the football pitch, but told himself not to be so stupid. After all, what could possibly go wrong?

The pitch was lined with students who had come to watch the game, some to show support to their friends, others as idle onlookers. Jack was encouraged to see Alfie and Callum standing there grinning at him, and he began to feel more hopeful. Marcus Littlewood was there too, and gave him a shy smile and a wave. He wondered whether Alison might also be there, but could not see her. Was she annoyed with him for not talking to her yesterday? Well, there would be plenty of time after the game. Whatever it was she had to say could surely wait until then.

Jack took his place and began limbering up. His eye fell upon Harvey Grahams' solid frame. He looked grim and ready for action. Jack looked around for Lucien but could not see him on the pitch. A sense of panic filled him. Where was he? He had promised to be there. The game was about to start at any moment now.

Mr. Cartwright stepped forward and lifted his whistle to his lips. The players stood rigid, waiting for the signal. A latecomer sauntered across the sideline. Jack breathed a sigh of relief; it was Lucien.

The whistle sounded and the game began. It got off to a fast and furious start, and for a while Jack forgot about Lucien and his instructions. First Harvey's team had the ball, then Jack's; now it had passed back to Harvey's. Up and down the pitch it went, with neither team scoring. Now Harvey had the ball and was making his way doggedly towards the goal. Jack pursued him, but to no avail; Harvey cut straight through the defence, aimed, kicked and landed the ball in the net. A cheer went up from the team and from a few of the spectators.

Play resumed, and this time Jack's team took possession of the ball. Jack ran ahead towards the goal; if he could shoot from here he would stand a good chance of scoring. The ball sped his way. He intercepted it and positioned himself before the goal. He raised his foot and aimed – a fraction of a second too late. An opponent flew past, taking the ball with him. It was Harvey. Less than a minute later the ball was heading his way again, but by now Jack had lost his opportunity. One of his team members aimed and scored.

"One all," shouted Mr. Cartwright, as the players resumed their positions. Jack was worried. Harvey was playing really well, and unless he found a way to defeat him soon he stood no chance of being selected for the team. Glancing up he caught Lucien's eye. The older boy winked at him and Jack's spirits rose. Maybe now was the time to put their plan into action.

The game continued at the same swift pace. No opportunity presented itself to tackle Harvey, and Jack was beginning to feel dispirited again. Then, out of nowhere, Harvey had taken the ball and was heading towards the goal. No-one seemed to be stopping him. Jack sped towards him and, as he approached Harvey, saw Lucien coming from the other direction. Lucien looked at Jack and nodded, his eyes glinting dangerously. Jack was almost upon Harvey; the ball was within reach. He extended his foot, and in the same instant Lucien tackled Harvey from behind. Harvey tumbled to the ground; the ball was in Jack's possession. He turned to face his own goal, but as he did so he heard an agonized cry. Harvey was sprawled across the pitch and Jack saw, to his horror, that Lucien was grinding his face into the mud with the spikes of his boots. He was striking him mercilessly.

Total confusion followed. The whistle blasted and Mr. Cartwright came rushing towards them. He knelt beside Harvey, who was motionless and white as a sheet, except for drops of blood trickling down his face. Players and spectators crowded in, and a hand was clamped firmly on Jack's shoulder. This was followed by more commotion as two teachers rushed to assistance, assessing whether an ambulance was required. It appeared that Harvey was unconscious.

Jack was appalled. It had all gone horribly wrong. He had wanted to teach Harvey a lesson and pay him back for his earlier assault, but had never intended to cause him serious harm. What on earth had possessed Lucien to kick him in the face in that vicious manner? That had never been part of the plan. He looked around for Lucien. A sea of faces swam before him, but he could see no sign of him.

Now he was being marched off by Mr. Cartwright, leaving the others to attend to Harvey.

"Is he OK?" Jack asked hoarsely.

"You'd better hope so," was the grim reply. "You've got a lot of explaining to do, young man."

Jack looked desperately again for Lucien, but he was nowhere to be seen.

Ten minutes later Jack found himself standing outside the headmaster's office. This was worse than any of the other trouble he had been in over the past few weeks. This was serious. He felt his fate was sealed when he discovered that the headmaster was away and that Mrs. Grimshaw, as deputy head, was in charge. She eyed him coldly as Mr. Cartwright gave an account of the incident, describing Jack's tackle followed by an evident physical assault on Harvey. He made no mention of Lucien's part in the event.

"Is this true, Jack?" Mrs. Grimshaw asked icily.

Jack swallowed. He hated the thought of informing on a fellow student, but did not see why he should take the blame for Lucien's actions.

"It's true that I ran up to Harvey and tackled him and got the ball off him. But I didn't trip him up – at least I don't think I did. It was Lucien who knocked him down and kicked him."

"Lucien?" exclaimed Mr. Cartwright. "Lucien who?"

"Lucien Ferndale," Jack answered, wondering at the sports teacher's incredulous face. "We both tackled Harvey at the same time."

Mr. Cartwright looked as if he were about to explode.

"I don't know what you think you're playing at, Jack Fletcher, but there was no Lucien Ferndale in the trials."

Now it was Jack's turn to look incredulous.

"But, sir," he blurted out wildly, "you must have seen him. He was playing on the same side as me. He came up to Harvey at exactly the same time as I did, and tackled him from behind. Then Harvey went down and Lucien started kicking him in the face. I never touched him, I swear."

A silence followed Jack's outburst. Mr. Cartwright looked as though he could not believe his ears, while Mrs. Grimshaw regarded them both stonily. Finally she spoke.

"It appears that you both have completely different stories, only one of which can possibly be true. Jack, I must warn you that lying in this situation is a very serious matter. You would be much better off telling the truth, however unpleasant the consequences, I can assure you."

"I am telling the truth," Jack cried, feeling desperate. How on earth could Mr. Cartwright not have seen Lucien?

"You insist that this boy Lucien was the one who injured Harvey?" Mrs. Grimshaw continued.

"Yes."

"And you, Mr. Cartwright, are sure that there was no student of that name playing in the trial?"

"Quite sure, Mrs. Grimshaw. In fact, I don't believe I've heard that name before. I don't know any student of that name."

"No, neither do I," Mrs. Grimshaw said thoughtfully. "What year would he be in?" This was addressed to Jack.

"I don't know, miss. Year Ten or Eleven, I should think. He's older than me."

Mrs. Grimshaw picked up the telephone.

"Hello, Julia. Could you do me a favour? Could you check through our records and see if we have a student by the name of Lucien Ferndale? Yes, that's right. Yes, L-U-C-I-E-N F-E-R-N-D-A-L-E. No, I'm not sure of the year. Many thanks."

The telephone rang two minutes later, but it was not the school secretary. It was news of Harvey.

"Well," Mrs. Grimshaw said, replacing the receiver, "it appears that Harvey Grahams is not seriously hurt. We may be thankful for that." This last remark seemed to be directed at Jack.

Jack said nothing. He felt some relief at the news, for despite his intense dislike of Harvey he had not wished him any serious harm. And the situation would have been even worse for him had Harvey been badly injured. But that did nothing to resolve the problem of Lucien.

A few minutes passed, which felt like hours, before the telephone rang a second time.

"Yes, hello, Julia." There was a pause. "You're quite sure?" Another pause. "Thank you for your help."

Mrs. Grimshaw's face was as hard as stone as she looked at Jack.

"Mrs. Norris has checked the records and there is no student by the name of Lucien Ferndale at this school."

Jack's mind was reeling. Surely this could not be happening.

"I'm not making it up. Please, you've got to believe me," Jack pleaded, trying desperately to think straight. "Maybe – Lucien Ferndale can't be his real name – that must be it." Suddenly he remembered something else. "He was in detention with me yesterday after school. The Ol— I mean, Miss Batstone was there. She would have seen him. Ask her."

Mrs. Grimshaw made no reply. She sat there, motionless as a statue, eyes fixed on him. Jack stared miserably at the floor, wishing it would open and swallow him up, so that he could disappear for good and leave this entire situation behind. He knew that Mrs. Grimshaw would never believe his word over Mr. Cartwright's. Jack had no reason to suppose that the sports teacher was deliberately lying, but he could not for the life of him understand how he could possibly have not seen Lucien. Yet, somehow, to Jack's severe misfortune, it appeared that he had not. His only hope now was that the scatty Old Bat would remember him and verify his story. He wished bitterly that he had never met Lucien – or whatever his real name was – or agreed to his stupid plan.

Mrs. Grimshaw, for her part, was equally at a loss. She had known Jack to be impertinent on occasions, but never capable of deliberate malice or barefaced deceit. This seemed totally out of character. And he seemed to be genuinely convinced by his story. On the other hand, Mr. Cartwright was both a reliable and trusted colleague. She had no reason to doubt his judgement or integrity; if he insisted he had not seen this boy, she was quite sure that was the case. Besides, there was no evidence that any Lucien Ferndale existed at the school. It just did not make sense.

She hoped that Miss Batstone could shed some light on the situation.

At length she spoke, in a slightly softer tone.

"Well, Jack. Have you anything more to say?"

Jack shook his head. "No, miss."

"Then I think we'll leave it there for today. But I must urge you, Jack," and her eyes glinted coldly, "to think very carefully about what has happened today, and if there is anything further that you would like to say, to come and see me straightaway. I need hardly remind you that this whole business is very serious, and I shall doubtless be speaking to you again. You may go now."

With a mumbled, "Yes, miss," and an embarrassed nod at Mr. Cartwright, Jack made a hasty exit. It was a relief to leave the stuffy room and escape Mrs. Grimshaw's piercing gaze, but nothing was resolved and his fate had been left undecided. He had started the day with such high hopes, he thought gloomily, and now it was with a heavy heart that he rejoined his classmates for the remainder of the afternoon.

Jack found the next two days a waking nightmare. News of the incident had spread throughout the school. Harvey Grahams was clearly making the most of his newly acquired celebrity status, exaggerating the assault on him and his resulting injuries for maximum effect and sympathy. Jack found himself cast as the villain of the piece. To his growing concern, nobody seemed to have witnessed Lucien's involvement in the whole affair. Even Alfie and Callum disbelieved his story. Jack described Lucien and his actions in meticulous detail, but his friends just shook their heads and stared at him as though he were mad.

"I don't know what you're on about, Jack," Callum admitted, completely bemused. "We were there the whole time, and the only person who tackled Harvey was you. There wasn't anyone else around."

Alfie had been staring at the ground and shuffling his feet uncomfortably during this conversation. Now he looked up and spoke hesitantly.

"We know you didn't mean to do it, Jack. It was an accident. But – well – you'd be better off just admitting it, you know."

Jack said nothing. What was the point? They did not believe him; nobody believed him. At least they were not shunning him, as everyone else seemed to be. He supposed he should be grateful for that.

Jack expected to be summoned to Mrs. Grimshaw's office at any moment, and was filled with a sense of dread every time he passed her in the corridor or, worse, faced her during history lessons. But to his surprise she did not appear to treat him any differently, and the summons did not come. Perhaps that was all part of her plan, to keep him in agonizing suspense.

Jack had not seen Alison since Tuesday morning, and wondered whether she was avoiding him too. He could not blame her. He had not been very nice to her that fateful day, and she was bound to have heard of his alleged assault in all its exaggerated detail. He would not blame her if she never spoke to him again. And yet, would she, *could* she, possibly be the one person who might just believe his story? They had shared an ordeal that no-one else could be expected to believe, and she had not doubted that his encounters with Celeste were real. It was a long shot, perhaps, but it had to be worth a try.

As soon as the bell rang, Friday lunchtime, Jack made his way to Alison's classroom. Year Nine students were streaming out of it and heading for the canteen. There was no sign of Alison among them, but he spotted a dark-haired girl whom he had seen talking to her on a few occasions.

"'Scuse me. Do you know where Alison is?"

The girl eyed him suspiciously. Her tone was hostile.

"Why? D'you want to beat her up as well?"

"No. I just want to talk to her, that's all."

There was a pause.

"I think she went to the library," the girl answered coldly, and walked off without another word. A few others glared at him and Jack's heart sank. Everyone was convinced he was a savage brute; why should Alison be any different? Nevertheless, he made his way to the library; at least it was in the opposite direction to the canteen, where the majority of the school was headed. He did not want to be around people right now, and people certainly did not seem to want him anywhere near them.

The library was empty. Jack threw his bag on the floor and slumped down in one of the chairs. Where else might Alison be? She was probably at lunch, along with everyone else. He gazed morosely at the neatly lined books on the shelves, and his eye fell upon an empty space. Three books lay in a heap on the floor, one of them open. They looked as though they had been dropped in a hurry. Curious, Jack moved closer to inspect them, stopping abruptly in his tracks. Was it his imagination or was there a shadow cast over them?

"Are you looking for Alison?" a familiar voice sounded behind him.

Startled, Jack spun around. He had not heard anyone enter the room. He was even more surprised when he saw who it was standing before him, tall and leering.

"Lucien! What are you doing here?" His initial shock turned to relief at seeing Lucien again, and then to anger. He opened his mouth to speak, but something in Lucien's demeanour forbade him to utter a word, much like their first meeting. He was even taller than Jack remembered, and leaner.

"Are you looking for Alison?" he repeated, towering over, his eyes narrowing, vivid green and penetrating. Jack had a fleeting sensation he had been in this situation once before. Dumbstruck, all he could do was nod and follow Lucien as he motioned him towards the door.

Once they reached the corridor outside, Jack felt a little bolder. There was something stifling about the library; here the air seemed fresher somehow. Lucien was striding at a great pace, and Jack had to run to keep up. However, he ventured to speak.

"Where've you been, Lucien? You just disappeared after the game on Tuesday."

Lucien did not answer. Jack tried again.

"I don't understand what's going on. Nobody seems to have seen you except me. Nobody believes you were there, that it was you that tackled Harvey Grahams. Mrs. Grimshaw said you're not even a student here."

This last comment succeeded in extracting a grim laugh from Lucien, but that was all. He continued striding with no change of pace. Jack was out of breath, but he was determined not to give up.

"Will you just tell me what's going on?"

"All in good time, Jack. All in good time."

Jack could get no more out of him, so reluctantly jogged along beside him, wondering where Lucien was leading him, but not liking to ask. They were moving away from the central part of the building, towards the east wing. They hurtled past the science labs, along a corridor and down a flight of stairs. Suddenly Lucien stopped, and his unpleasant expression unnerved Jack. They were alone. He waited for Lucien to speak, but the taller boy just looked at him for a minute or two. He seemed to be sizing him up, and Jack fidgeted uncomfortably, avoiding his penetrating gaze. When he finally spoke his tone had changed. It sounded softer and friendlier.

"You don't really want to look for Alison, do you? She hasn't given you a moment's peace since you met her. And things will only get worse – she'll drag you deeper and deeper into things you don't want to get into, with all her crazy ideas. And what about your mates? They're not sure what to make of you right now. Do you want them to end up thinking you're as crazy as she is?"

Jack started. What was Lucien – a mind reader? He could not deny those thoughts had crossed his mind. But how on earth did Lucien know what had gone on between them?

Lucien seemed to sense he had struck a chord, and smiled, continuing, "You can still walk away from all this, Jack."

"And do what?"

"Hang out with me. I'll show you a much better time."

Lucien leant against the wall, hands in his pockets, supremely confident. For a moment Jack tried to imagine what it would be like to be his friend, strutting around the school without a care, cool and confident, quashing bullies left, right and centre. It was a tempting prospect. But that was not the way things had turned out so far.

"Hang on a sec – it's because of you I've got into all this trouble. It was your idea to tackle Harvey Grahams, and I'm the one that's got all the blame for it!"

Lucien laughed quietly.

"Well, it was worth it, wasn't it? We taught that little thug a lesson. He won't be making it into the football team now."

"No, and neither will I!" Jack retorted. "So it hasn't done me much good, has it?"

Lucien smiled again, secretively.

"Well, there are plenty of other ways."

Jack looked at him sharply. His tone was casual, but Jack did not trust him. There seemed to be callousness, even cruelty, concealed beneath the cool exterior. The image of Lucien grinding Harvey's face mercilessly into the mud came back to him in a flash, and he wavered no longer.

"No thanks. I don't know who you are, Lucien Ferndale, but I wish I'd never met you. Just tell me where Alison is and leave me alone."

Lucien sucked his breath in, giving his thin face a pinched look. His green eyes glinted maliciously.

"Well, well," he sneered. "I thought you had more guts than that, Jack Fletcher. I was obviously wrong."

Now Jack's blood was boiling.

"Guts! You can talk about guts! You're the one that set me up and then disappeared off, leaving me to take all the flak. And

pulverizing Harvey to a pulp didn't show guts. That was just—"
He broke off, searching for the right word.

"Mean? Cruel? Underhand?" Lucien suggested indifferently. Jack made no reply. Suddenly Lucien laughed out loud, a grim, determined laugh, and strode off again. Jack followed him uncertainly. Part of him wanted to run back in the opposite direction, but he had come this far, and he did want to talk to Alison, if she would listen to him. They were winding their way through a longer corridor towards the older classrooms that had fallen into disuse. What was Alison doing over here? Or did Lucien have some other trick up his sleeve? He stopped, feeling suddenly afraid. The place was silent and the air smelt stale. Lucien had shown no qualms about beating up another boy for no apparent reason; what if he was about to do the same to him?

"Not so sure of yourself now?" Lucien hissed, and grabbing Jack roughly by the shoulder, thrust him forward.

"Where are we going? Where's Alison?"

"Oh, Alison!" Lucien placed both his hands on Jack's shoulders and leant down until his eyes were almost level with Jack's. They bored into his, unblinking. "You're much too late for Alison!"

"What do you mean?" faltered Jack, seized with a sudden panic.

In response, Lucien flung open an old classroom door, pushed Jack inside, and slammed the door shut behind them. Jack froze. Three dark figures stood before him, shrouded in shadows. An unmistakable stench filled the room. The figures were bending over something – or someone. As Jack leant forward for a closer look his blood ran cold. There, lying motionless on the floor, deathly white, was Alison.

Behind him Lucien let out a roar of laughter, a sound Jack would never forget. It was a diabolical laugh of pure evil. Lucien stepped forward, and it seemed to Jack he had grown even taller since entering the room. As Jack watched, horror-struck, he continued to grow, until his head almost reached the ceiling. His arms hung long and dangling by his side, while his hands doubled in size, revealing talon-like nails. Lucien's skin was changing colour; it was growing darker and no longer resembled human flesh. His face became narrower, more pointed, and the slits of his eyes were a venomous green. A menacing grin stretched across his lean face. The transformation was complete.

"Now do you know who I am, Jack?" he hissed.

10

In the Meadow

Jack stood, petrified, staring at the demon in front of him. It was blocking his way to Alison, but now the other three figures turned to face him too. Slowly, they moved forward to join their comrade, and Jack found himself face to face with four creatures of Darkness, each as monstrous as the other. They were leering and slavering horribly, green slime oozing from their parted lips. The stench was intolerable. They were closing in on him now, a wall of darkness. Jack thought he was going to pass out.

Then suddenly he remembered. Of course – the nails! He thrust his hand into his blazer pocket. *It was empty.* He tried the other pocket, but only pulled out a crumpled tissue. The nails were not there.

"Where are they?" he thought wildly. He must have lost them somehow, probably in all the excitement of the football trial.

There was nothing more he could do. Surrounded by darkness, Jack closed his eyes and waited for the end. He could feel the demons' odorous breath on his neck as they hissed and spluttered, and the stench made him retch. Any moment now they would be bearing down on him, their monstrous hands around his neck, ready to squeeze all life out of him. They had already got Alison. Now it was his turn.

But the end did not come. From the opposite side of the room came a sudden noise. Bizarrely, it sounded like the blast of a trumpet. Whatever it was, it startled the demons. A tall figure stood in the corner, clothed in white, with golden streaming hair, brandishing a gleaming sword. Another figure, similarly attired, appeared from behind the first, followed by a third. Each carried a sword and shield. The demons hissed venomously, but Jack noticed a look of fear in their eyes.

With a loud cry the three warriors leapt forward. The demons writhed and spluttered and turned to face their enemy. Jack's knees buckled and he fell, crumpled, to the floor. The warriors in white drew their swords and advanced, as one. Their movements were as graceful as a dancer's, but their faces were set like flint, and a fury blazed in their eyes. The demons arched their backs, spitting and screeching. One of them lurched towards their aggressors, but one stroke from the flashing sword sent it into rapid retreat. It crouched, cowering in a corner, nursing a wound across its lean chest.

This seemed to spur the other three on to attack. Teeth bared, they hurled themselves at the warriors, and a raging battled ensued. Jack watched, aghast, as the hissing beasts leapt at their enemies, striking them with their clawed talons, their pointed tails crashing down on their legs like whips. The warriors showed no signs of fear, however. In one deft movement they had positioned their shining shields to ward off the attack, so that the monstrous talons flailed fruitlessly, and the tails lashed in a futile frenzy, striking angrily at the floor. The presence of the shields seemed to have quite an effect on the demons; they retreated a few paces, a renewed expression of fear on their hideous faces.

Now it was the warriors' turn to attack. With a terrifying cry they advanced again, moving as one man, swords held aloft. Jack gasped at their swift, fluid motion and dazzling swordsmanship. The demons fought back, but were no match for them. Within minutes they found themselves surrounded, the sharp blades thrust towards their throats. But at this moment, the fourth demon, which until now had remained cowering in its corner, suddenly lunged forward and leapt at the nearest warrior with a howl of rage. Its slavering jaw was wide open, revealing deadly fangs that were bared, ready to tear the white flesh into shreds. In an instant the warrior had turned, and even as the beast had risen to its full height, poised to strike, he raised his arm and plunged his sword into its belly. A deafening scream reverberated around the room, and the creature crashed to the floor. As swift as lightning, the warrior lifted his sword above his head. Jack watched the glittering blade dive downwards, and before he realized what had happened, the demon's ghastly head was rolling towards him, severed clean from its body. It was a horrific sight: bloodshot eyes wide and staring, mouth gaping open from which emerged a huge tongue, lolling sideways, black and lifeless. Jack swallowed hard in an effort to prevent himself from vomiting. The other demons let out a shriek of terror, and flailed wildly around. With a triumphant roar the warriors were upon them, shields flashing and swords ablaze. The demons were defeated, and within minutes their putrid carcasses lay sprawled in a smouldering heap.

The warriors issued a cry of victory, and suddenly the room was filled with a brilliant light. The tallest figure, the one who had slain the first demon, now turned towards Jack. His heart missed a beat as he saw its features for the first time: translucent skin, penetrating eyes, mouth set firm; it was unmistakably Celeste.

At that moment a fear seized him, far more terrible than his fear of the demons. The light was unbearable, burning through his skin to the very core of his being. He felt filthy and repugnant. He could not look at that radiant face, could not meet those terrifying eyes. He had no place here among such dazzling splendour. He had to get out. Fast. Now. Jack shakily struggled to his feet and, shielding his eyes, stumbled, trembling, towards the door. He half-staggered, half-ran along the deserted corridors back through the school and out into the playground. Not until the school gate was some distance behind him did he finally pause for breath. Where to now? He could not go back to school and did not want to go home. Without really knowing where he was heading, he continued along the path at the same frenzied pace, oblivious to the passers-by. He had never in his life felt so alone.

A dim memory surfaced, and suddenly he recalled Celeste standing before him, not in the formidable splendour he had just witnessed, but casual in jeans and trainers. Her words came back to him: "If you ever lose your way completely, come back here, where you started." There was only one place he could go. Taking a deep breath and a right turn, he set off resolutely towards the meadows. He felt little relief, however, in reaching them. He was still left with himself, the one person from whom he could not escape. It was with a heavy heart that Jack retraced his earlier steps to find the spot where Celeste had taken him only a week ago. How different everything had seemed then, his adventure lying before him like freshly fallen snow unsullied by footprints. Now it lay muddied and spoilt; he had failed miserably and ruined everything. How could he have allowed himself to get sidetracked by Lucien? Why hadn't he listened to Alison when she had tried to tell him what was happening? It was too late now; Celeste would want nothing more to do with him, he was sure of that. And Alison? Jack shuddered and sank to the ground. He saw her motionless body before him, and he feared the worst. If only he had listened to her, he might have reached her before the demons had. In one respect Lucien had been right: he had been far too late.

His feeling of filthiness was growing in intensity. What was he doing here, contaminating this place? Jack hid his face in his hands and began sobbing uncontrollably. He did not know how long he remained in that position of utter despair. At first he was only conscious of his convulsed sobs, and the bitter tears which flowed freely, but did nothing to wash away his grime.

After a while Jack became aware that a silence had fallen. He cautiously removed his hands from his face and looked up. A great stillness filled the air, as though another presence had descended. He had an uncanny feeling that the rustling of leaves and grass had been silenced, and the movement of even the smallest insects stilled by it. It was almost as though the natural world were standing to attention in the presence of some greater power.

Jack waited. And then a voice whispered in his ear, "Don't be afraid." He started and turned. There was no-one there; the meadow was deserted. Perhaps he had imagined it? But there it was again: "Don't be afraid. I am with you." It was a gentle, soothing voice, like the breeze ruffling a young bird's feathers, or the ripples in a pond, or a mother comforting a small child, and yet, like none of these. It was something even gentler, and even stronger.

"But, but—" Jack faltered, his face buried in his hands once more; he dared not raise his eyes. "I've messed everything up." He blurted the words out. They seemed so inadequate, but what more was there to say? A searing pain tore through him, as though a knife were twisting in his stomach, slicing through his chest and stabbing him right in the heart. He was shaking uncontrollably. Never in his life had he felt so weak, so dirty and so helpless. Through muffled sobs he stammered hoarsely, "I – I'm sorry. Please – please – help me."

As soon as he uttered the words, a change swept over him. The stabbing pain in his chest was replaced with a new sensation of warmth from somewhere in the pit of his stomach slowly spreading through his body, until he felt a delicious tingling in his fingers and toes. At the same time he felt a pressure on his shoulders, firm yet gentle. Something – or someone – seemed to be lifting him carefully from his prone position to his knees, then gradually to his feet, until Jack finally stood upright, bathed in wonderful warmth. It was more than warmth; his whole body – no, his entire being – felt light, lighter than he had ever felt before, as though every weight, every problem, every worry and every mistake he had ever made had just melted away. And he no longer felt dirty. The warm glow emanating through him, whatever it was, had removed all trace of filth. He felt light and clean – and free.

Jack could never fully articulate this experience. He just knew that he was not alone. The gentle whisper, the hand on his shoulder, the stillness now as he stood there, feeling more alive than he had ever felt before, all spoke of Someone's presence – Someone who had been watching him; Someone who rose above his fears and failures and foibles; but Someone who still cared. And somehow Jack knew too that the past no longer mattered; he had been freed from it – forgiven, even. He could go forward and continue his journey with renewed strength and courage.

He had met the Master.

11

More Questions Than Answers

Jack was in no hurry to leave. Bathed in the warmth and tranquillity of his surroundings, he felt as though he could stay there forever. Every tree, flower, even each blade of grass, seemed somehow more vibrant in colour, more intricate in detail. Birdsong filled the air in wonderfully varied melody. Jack leant against the trunk of a tree and looked up at the branches overhead, sunlight filtering through the leaves and casting speckled shadows on to the grass beneath. In an impulse, he kicked off his shoes and pulled off his socks, allowing his feet to sink into the cool grass, its softness contrasting with the firmness of the bark against his back. His senses were heightened. He could see, hear, smell, touch things in a way that he never had before: shades of colour, fragrances, birdsong blending in harmony. He could almost taste the newly awakened atmosphere of the place, brimming with life. It was marvellous. But most wonderful of all was the feeling of joy that was bubbling up inside him and threatening to burst out of his chest, together with an incredible sense of peace that infused his whole being. If only he could feel this way forever!

Eventually, it was time to return home. Jack strode through the streets with a new lightness of step, whistling. The town too seemed to be vibrant with life. In the distance he heard a clock chime four.

Four o'clock! Jack started, as he realized with a shock that he had missed the entire afternoon's lessons. He had lost all sense of time from the moment he had entered the disused classroom. How was he going to explain his absence? He could not afford to get into any more trouble. Oh well, he would worry about that on Monday – he had the whole weekend ahead of him now.

Jack's second shock occurred as he turned the corner into his road to see a fair-haired figure in school uniform standing at the end of his garden path. Jack stopped in his tracks and his heart skipped a beat. Alison! She was still alive! She had survived her horrific ordeal. His first instinct was to run towards her, but then a surge of fear gripped him. He had deserted her when she had needed him most. She had nearly been killed by the hideous demons, and he had done nothing to stop them. How could he possibly face her now? How could he ever face her again? Jack felt his newly acquired sense of peace seeping away as the enormity of the situation took hold. He wondered whether she had spotted him yet; perhaps he could turn back and find somewhere to hide until she had gone? His thoughts were interrupted by a sudden movement.

"Jack!" She was running towards him.

Jack stood rooted to the spot, immobilized.

"Jack!" To his astonishment, Alison ran right up to him and flung her arms around him. "Oh, Jack! You're OK!"

Stunned, Jack stared at her incredulously.

"Yeah, I'm OK," he faltered. "But what about you? Are you all right?"

She nodded. "Yes, I'm fine now." They stood there awkwardly for a moment, neither knowing what to do or say next. So much had happened to them both since they had last spoken, that it was difficult to know where – or how – to start. Jack was acutely aware of how badly he had let Alison down, so much so that he could not look her in the eye, but stared down at the ground, a knot tightening in his stomach. He tried to form some words of apology, but none came. A gentle pressure on his shoulder made him start.

"Jack, it's OK."

"What?" Jack looked up into Alison's earnest blue eyes. Her hand was resting on his shoulder and she was smiling.

"Honestly – it's all OK."

"But – but – I wouldn't talk to you – I got sidetracked by that stupid football trial and – and – him." Jack couldn't bring himself to mention Lucien's name. "And then – and then – I was too late – I did come looking for you – but I was too late – they – they'd already – got you." He felt dangerously close to tears. "I'm sorry."

"I know you are. And it's really OK. It's over now, and I'm all right. And so are you." This last sentence was uttered with a sigh of relief, which Jack found touching. She had clearly been worried about him too.

"I've got so much to tell you, Jack. Could we go in?" Alison gestured towards Jack's house.

"Oh, yeah. Course." He walked up the path and opened the front door, Alison following behind. His mum was in the kitchen, peeling potatoes. She turned to greet him and, finding her son with a girl in tow, quickly changed her look of surprise to a welcoming smile.

"Hello, Jack. Hello..."

"I'm Alison," Alison said quickly. "Hello, Mrs. Fletcher, nice to meet you."

"Alison's from school," Jack stated by way of explanation, rather pointlessly as she was wearing the navy blazer and tie of St Michael's.

"Nice to meet you too, Alison. Are you in the same class as Jack?"

"No, I'm in Year Nine."

"Oh?" Another look of surprise – and a touch of concern, Jack noted – with mild amusement. "Well, would you like to stay for tea?"

"Oh, no – thank you – that's very kind, but my mum'll be expecting me home soon. I've just come around for a – er – quick chat with Jack."

"Oh. Right." For a moment his mum seemed lost for words. She looked at Jack enquiringly, but he merely shrugged. "Well, I'm sure you'd both like a drink, wouldn't you? And a biscuit? I've got some chocolate Hobnobs somewhere." She hurriedly rummaged in the kitchen cupboards, and two minutes later had produced a tray with two glasses of juice and a plate of biscuits.

"Thanks, Mum. We'll just be upstairs."

"Er – OK then."

Jack led the way upstairs to his bedroom and kicked the door open. He guessed from the sound of the television coming from the lounge that his sister was happily occupied, so they shouldn't be disturbed. He looked at Alison, feeling suddenly shy.

"So, where do we start?"

"You go first," she answered eagerly.

"Shouldn't it be ladies first?" Jack retorted, with a rueful attempt at humour. Alison looked at him archly.

"Bit late to play the gentleman now, isn't it?"

Jack blushed, but there was a twinkle in her eye that reassured him she was only teasing. He reached for a chocolate biscuit, bit it thoughtfully and, hesitantly at first, recounted the events of the last week: his encounter with Lucien, the fateful football trial, his grilling from Mrs. Grimshaw, Lucien's terrible transformation, and the raging battle between the warriors and the demons. He struggled as the images of the horrific incident flooded into his vision: the hideous, deadly demons; the terrifying warriors; the blinding light; and there, in the midst of it all, Alison's motionless body. But, as painful as it was to relive and relate this incident, Jack found it even harder to describe the events that had followed in the meadow. After all, he had not actually seen anything, he had merely sensed it; yet it had been so undeniably real. And it had been such an intensely personal experience that it was very difficult to convey it to somebody else. Would Alison even believe his story? Did she think he had imagined the whole thing?

Jack paused, waiting for her to speak, but she said nothing at first. Then, after a minute or two's silence, she murmured, "Wow. You've met the Master too." Then, with mounting excitement, "That's amazing! Fantastic! Jack, this makes all the difference!"

"Does it?"

"Of course! Don't you see what it means? We're not on our own in this, Jack – the Master's helping us. He's already sent Celeste and those other two messengers to help us, but now that you've actually met him yourself, you've got some of his power inside you – and so have I. He'll show us what we need to do next – he's got it all under control. And, what's more, he's with us – he'll be with us every step of the way."

Jack was momentarily silent. He knew he had got himself into something big, something outside the realms of his own experience and control, the moment he had accepted Celeste's invitation. But he had had no idea just how huge this strange quest, if that was what he should call it, was. Just a few hours ago he had felt so utterly forsaken and alone – more alone than he had ever felt in his life. But he realized now that he had never been alone. Celeste had come. Then he had met Alison. And Celeste had returned, with reinforcements to rescue Alison in her hour of need. Hadn't she said she would be keeping a watch on him? Then just as he thought he had blown it and was running away, the Master had come and found him too. And brought him back. Back into this adventure, back into the journey they were on which, now they had started, they could not stop until they reached the end – wherever that might be.

He looked up at Alison, and now it was his voice that was eager.

"So, go on then. Your turn – what have you been up to?"

"Well..." Alison took a deep breath. "After we last spoke (she delicately refrained from saying, "After you wouldn't speak to me," Jack noted gratefully), I went back to the library. I'd been back a couple of times since – you know – since we were both there. I just had this odd feeling that there was something going on there. I mean, there must have been a reason why that – demon thing – was in there before."

Jack nodded, privately impressed that Alison had had the courage to go back there after that demonic beast had attacked her.

"So, anyway," she continued, "the first time not much seemed to be happening. There were a couple of Year Elevens studying in the corner. Then two Year Ten girls came in and started looking through the bookshelves. I don't know why, but there seemed to be something a bit odd about them and the way that they were looking – almost as if they were desperate to find whatever book they were after."

"Who were they?"

"I don't know their names. One's quite tall, with dark hair and glasses. The other one's smaller, with hair a bit like mine, only shorter."

"So did they find what they were looking for?"

"No. They scoured the entire library then went out again without a single book. It was a bit weird really." She broke off, lost in thought.

"And?" Jack urged. "So what happened after that?"

"Nothing more, that day," continued Alison. "But I have seen those two girls around the school since and – oh, I don't know – I may be imagining things, but it's just a feeling I get."

"What? What feeling?"

"Well, there just looks something odd about them. Almost as if there's a shadow or something hanging over them. And when I passed them in the corridor the other day one of them – the tall one with the dark hair – gave me a really dirty look."

"Do you think they've got something to do with the Darkness?"

"I don't know, but I think they might have. There's just something about them that's not right. And there's more, Jack. I went back to the library again a couple of days later. As soon as I opened the door I knew something wasn't right; this really creepy feeling came over me. There was a group sitting around the table in the corner – there must have been about six of them – mostly Year Nines and Tens."

"Did you know any of them?"

"One of the girls I saw before was there – the other one, the one with the blonde hair. And a couple of boys in my year – Craig Douglas and Freddie Marks. And a boy in your class – the one that you had all that trouble with – what's his name – Harry Grahams, is it?"

"Harvey," Jack corrected grimly. "I might have known he'd be involved if there's something dodgy going on. I wouldn't trust him as far as I could throw him."

"Anyway," Alison continued, "they were all huddled around the table, whispering. There was no-one else in there, and when I came in, they all shut up, just like that. There was this really creepy silence, and some of them were staring at me as if I had two heads or something. Even Craig and Freddie, who I get on all right with, were pretending they hadn't seen me, I could tell. I wasn't sure what to do – I felt like going out again – but there was no way I was going to let them intimidate me. So I just casually started looking through the bookshelves. I could see out of the corner of my eye they had a big thick book open in the middle of the table, and it felt as though they were crowding around it, almost as if they were trying to stop me from seeing it, like they were protecting it, somehow. I couldn't get any closer without making it obvious I was watching them, so I went behind the bookshelf where they couldn't see me. I could hear them whispering, but I couldn't hear what they were actually saying – they were being really careful not to let me hear, I'm sure of it. They were hiding something – I could tell from the secretive looks on their faces, and the way they were huddled together. They didn't stay for much longer after that, though. I'm sure they knew I was wondering what they were up to, because they all got up together and went out without a word. It was really weird."

"Did you see the book they were reading?"

Alison shook her head regretfully. "No, 'fraid not. They took it with them. But listen to this, Jack. I waited for a few minutes to make sure they had gone, and when I came out and went up to the table there was a shadow covering the middle of it, right where the book had been."

"Are you sure?"

Alison nodded vigorously. "Absolutely. And it wasn't anything to do with where the light was coming in through the window, Jack – it wasn't a normal shadow. The chairs and the rest of the table weren't in shadow – just where the book had been. It must have been – well – a *dark* shadow, you know what I mean?"

Jack nodded. A tingling sensation slowly crept up his spine and his heart beat a little faster.

"And there's something else, Jack. I was just about to open the door to go out, when I noticed the wastepaper bin in the corner. There was a shadow sort of hovering over it. I swear to you, Jack, I'm not making it up – it was definitely there." Her eyes were wide and earnest.

"I felt really scared," Alison continued, "but I went up to the bin, and this horrible cold, clammy feeling came over me – really creepy, it was. I thought my heart was going to explode, it was beating so hard. There was nothing inside it except one scrunched-up piece of paper."

"Have you got it?" Jack's mouth was slightly dry.

In response, Alison opened her bag and produced a carefully folded piece of paper which appeared to have been previously screwed up and discarded.

"Here." She handed it to Jack. He took it and unfolded it without speaking. On the paper was a crude drawing of what looked like a vampire bat, with outstretched wings and protruding fangs, but on which, somewhat bizarrely, had been drawn a pair of glasses over the glaring eyes. Underneath were three letters, written in capitals:

M.A.B.

"M.A.B." Jack read aloud slowly. "What do you suppose that means?"

Alison shrugged. "I've no idea. But I'm sure it's got something to do with them and that book they were looking at, whatever it is that they're up to. I reckon one of them must have thrown this paper in the bin on their way out."

"So when did you find this?" Jack enquired, staring at the strange sketch and letters below, as though looking at it longer would somehow reveal some hidden meaning.

"Three days ago. That's what I wanted to show you that day – before – you know..."

"Yeah." Jack did not want to ask his next question, but knew he had to hear Alison's story to its conclusion. He swallowed painfully. "Did you go back to the library today?"

"I was going to. I was on my way there at lunchtime, when I passed the two Year Ten girls again in the corridor. I waited until they'd gone by, then turned back and followed them. I kept my distance, and I don't think they saw me – they were too busy whispering together to notice anyone else. I followed them past the science block, but by the time I'd got around the corner, they'd gone. I don't know what they were doing down that end of the school – it's pretty much deserted. Anyway, I carried on going, and then got that creepy feeling back again – a sort of tingling down my spine. There was no-one about, but I really felt as though I wasn't alone. I kept going towards the old art room at the end, and it suddenly felt darker – as though someone had switched a light off, although there was no light on in the first place. I couldn't see any definite shadow; it just felt darker all around. Then I heard a sound coming from the classroom, and thought maybe the girls had gone in there."

Alison paused, turning very pale. Jack wanted to say something reassuring, but his own throat felt tight and no words would come. After an awkward minute or two, Alison spoke slowly and softly.

"The door was shut. I could feel my hand trembling as I turned the handle. The creepy feeling was getting worse all the time. I went inside, expecting to see the two girls and maybe some of the others in the group. But the room was completely dark, and there was no sign of anyone. There was a horrible smell – not a musty smell you'd normally get from a room that's not been used for a while – but something much stronger. It made me feel sick. And then – then—" She paused again, and shuddered. She took a deep breath and, with an effort, forced herself to continue.

"I saw a shadow on the wall opposite. It started at the skirting board, and seemed to grow until it reached the ceiling. And then the same thing happened on the walls either side, so that these three huge shadows were practically filling all three walls. They were horrible, Jack; I was so scared. I wanted to run but I couldn't. My feet wouldn't move. I couldn't even open my mouth to scream. Nothing. Then they started to change shape, all together. I saw their heads appear, and their arms and legs – they looked just like that monster in the library, but three of them. And last of all their eyes – evil, green eyes – all staring at me as though they wanted to kill me. They started moving towards me, all at the same time. I just stood there; I was petrified. I could feel their breath on me – it was foul. Then they were closing in on me. Their breath was stronger; I was about to pass out. I can't remember any more after that. The last thing I saw was their three pairs of eyes glaring down at me.

"When I came to, the room was filled with light. It was almost blinding, it was so bright. I didn't know where I was for a minute or two, and I hardly dared open my eyes. When I did finally look up there was someone different standing in front of me – not any of the demons any more, but a girl. At least, she sort of looked like a girl, but not like a normal girl, not like anyone I'd ever seen before, if that makes sense. She was wearing a long white robe, right down to her feet, and her hair was actually shining, as though it were made of gold. And she had really white skin – almost like snow. She didn't look like a real person; I thought I must be dreaming, at first."

"Celeste," Jack interjected.

"Really?" Alison's eyes widened with wonder. "She didn't tell me her name, but I know that she was one of the Master's messengers. There were three of them, all dressed in white and in armour. Their faces were gleaming – almost too bright to look at. I was afraid of them at first. But then the first one – Celeste, you say – knelt down and held out her hand to me. She was smiling, and there was something calm and gentle and sort of peaceful about her. She helped me up."

"And you were OK?" Jack asked anxiously. "You weren't hurt?"

"No, amazingly. I was a bit shaken up and I had a cut on my leg, but I wasn't badly injured. I think they must have come just in time, before those other things got me. Another few minutes and – well – I don't really want to think about what might have happened."

"No, me neither," Jack added quickly.

"Anyway," Alison continued briskly, in a brighter tone, "I saw that Celeste had a bottle in her hand, and the next thing I knew, she was dabbing some sort of ointment on my cuts and bruises. I don't know what it was, but it was incredible; I was healed instantly. In fact, I feel better than I did before they hurt me – good as new, as they say!"

"Did she speak to you? Celeste?" Jack was eager to know.

"Yeah, she did. Not at first, though. After she'd put the ointment stuff on me she just sort of stood there looking at me. I felt a bit uncomfortable to be honest – it was almost as though she was looking right inside me – into my mind, into my thoughts. I didn't really like it. Then eventually she smiled at me and said, "You're ready.""

"And?" Jack prompted.

"That's it. 'You're ready.' That's all she said."

Jack shifted somewhat uncomfortably.

"She didn't – she didn't mention me at all, did she?" he asked hesitantly.

"No, she didn't. And I didn't even know you'd been there in the room."

"Oh." Jack felt a sense of disappointment. He was not sure what he had expected; he had half-feared some rebuke, half-hoped for a word of encouragement, or at least some indication of what was happening and what they should do next. But there was nothing. Just, "You're ready." Ready for what exactly? And what about him? Did Celeste think he was ready for whatever lay ahead? Or had she given up on him? She *had* known he was there in the classroom – she had looked straight at him. He had been too terrified and too ashamed to speak to her. But that had been before he had met the Master in the meadows. Everything had changed for him too.

Jack's reverie was interrupted as Alison gave an abrupt start.

"Oh – look at the time! I'd better go – my mum'll be wondering where I am."

They walked down the stairs in silence, both absorbed with their own thoughts, having heard each other's stories. As they headed for the front door, the living room door opened and Lucy appeared in the hallway.

"Hi, Jack." Her smile froze as she saw Alison following behind him.

"Hello," Alison said brightly. "It's Lucy, isn't it? I'm Alison."

Lucy did not reply, but glowered at the pair of them.

"Charming!" Jack muttered sarcastically as he opened the door for his friend, giving his sister a disdainful sideways glance. He returned to his bedroom. The piece of paper that Alison had shown him was lying on the floor where he had left it. He picked it up and scrutinized it again.

M.A.B. What on earth could it mean?

12

M.A.B.

Lucy was uncharacteristically quiet as they sat down for dinner that evening. Jack did not mind; it meant he could think in peace. Or at least, he would have been able to had his mum not badgered him with questions about Alison. How had he met her? How long had he known her? Where did she live? Who were her friends?

"It's all right, Mum, she's not my girlfriend!" he burst out finally, in exasperation. "She's just a friend."

Lucy snorted across the table. Jack eyed her suspiciously.

"Have you got a problem with Alison?" he demanded. "You were really rude to her when she left just now – you wouldn't even say hello."

A dark expression clouded Lucy's face as she muttered into her plate of pasta.

"I don't like her."

"Why on earth not? Do you even know her?" Jack asked accusingly.

Lucy shrugged and lifted a forkful of pasta to her mouth. She evidently had nothing more to say. Feeling nettled, but reluctant to start an argument, Jack turned his attention to his own dinner. His mother, however, appeared less willing to let things go. She now began questioning him about school life in general. How was he getting on in his lessons? How was he finding the workload in Year Eight? Was anything worrying him?

Jack was bemused. She looked concerned, although she was trying to sound casual, and she had barely touched her meal. He did not have to wait long to discover what lay behind her questioning.

After they had finished eating and cleared the table, and Lucy had retreated upstairs to her bedroom, his mum asked quietly, "Jack, could I have a word, please?"

This sounded ominous. He reluctantly followed her into the lounge and sat down warily in the armchair. He did not want to be talking to his mother right now; he wanted to be alone to think through all the events of the past few days and to figure out what he and Alison should do next. His mum was perched upright on the edge of the sofa, a folded piece of paper in her hand.

"Jack, I received a letter from school today."

Jack's heart sank. So this was it. After leaving him in suspense for the past week, his recent trouble had finally caught up with him. Mrs. Grimshaw must have written to his mum to tell her all about the incident at the football trial, and doubtless all his other misdemeanours as well.

Jack's fears were confirmed. Mrs. Grimshaw had done exactly that, and it did not make pleasant reading. He squirmed as his mum read the letter aloud, looking at him reproachfully. He wished she would yell at him; that would have been easier to endure, and at least it would have been over and done with. But instead she seemed to want to dissect and scrutinize every minute detail in her efforts to understand her son's wayward behaviour. Worst of all, they had been summoned to a meeting with the deputy head teacher herself in order to discuss the matter further.

Eventually his mum finished. Jack hated seeing her so upset, and hated even more the fact he was responsible. She left the room, fighting back tears, leaving the letter lying there. Jack had no wish to re-read it, but his eye settled on the signature at the bottom of the page, cold, precise and efficient, like everything about Mrs. Grimshaw.

Margery A. B. Grimshaw
Deputy Head Teacher

Margery A. B. Grimshaw. *M.A.B.* His heart quickened.

Jack scarcely slept that night. His mind was reeling from all that had happened during the past week, and he found his thoughts darting from Lucien and the football trial, to his grilling in Mrs. Grimshaw's office, to Alison, back to Lucien and the other demons, to Celeste and her fellow warriors, to the library and Alison's discoveries there, to the imminent meeting with his mother and Mrs. Grimshaw, and the discovery that her initials matched those on the cryptic piece of paper Alison had found. And as these thoughts raced back and forth through his mind, Jack experienced a rollercoaster of emotions: horror mingled with relief, following Alison's narrow escape; anger and shame; mounting excitement that he may have found the key to unlocking the mystery surrounding the shadowy activities that were clearly taking place; then a plummeting sense of fear as his summons to the deputy head teacher loomed large. But through this frenetic cycle of feelings, one thing dominated: the hand on his shoulder, the strong yet gentle voice, "Don't be afraid. I am with you." And once again, Jack was suffused with a sense of peace and a certainty that everything would somehow work out. When he eventually fell asleep, it was not the shadows, perplexities and troubles that pervaded his dreams, but the calm and stillness of the meadow.

Jack awoke the next morning feeling remarkably refreshed. As he sat down to breakfast, his mum's wan expression suggested she had not slept so well. She sipped her coffee in near silence, tight-lipped and tense. Lucy, also, did not quite seem herself. Her face too looked a little pale, and there were dark rings under her eyes. She ate her bowl of cornflakes in a somewhat distracted fashion.

Jack could hardly wait to get to school and share his latest discovery with Alison. He scanned the playground impatiently, searching for her among the throngs of uniformed boys and girls who stood chatting as they waited for the morning bell to summon them to lessons. Turning a corner into a smaller, more secluded courtyard, he stopped abruptly. A group of about six or seven students stood huddled together, talking intently in low voices. Jack saw two girls who fitted Alison's description of the Year Ten girls she had previously encountered in the library. Harvey Grahams was also there – as arrogant as ever, Jack thought bitterly, although with an uncharacteristic intensity in his usually dull features. Suddenly, Jack's heart missed a beat as he recognized a smaller girl in the middle of the group, craning her neck as she leant forward eagerly to hear what was being said. It was Lucy.

What was his sister doing, getting mixed up with this crowd? He wanted to run over and pull her away, out of their clutches, away from whatever it was they were dragging her into. Just as these thoughts were racing through his mind, Harvey turned and smiled at him, a sneering, contemptuous, self-satisfied smile, that seemed to be daring Jack to step forward. Jack stood irresolutely, fists clenched. A restraining hand on his arm made him start.

"Hi, Jack."

"What? Oh – it's you. Hi, Alison."

She followed his gaze and shook her head.

"Come on, Jack. He's not worth it."

"I know. But she is." He nodded in the direction of his sister, and Alison let out a gasp.

"Lucy! What's she doing with that lot?"

"That's what I'd like to know," Jack muttered through gritted teeth, still glaring at Harvey, who had turned his focus back to the group and seemed to be paying Lucy special attention, hands thrust nonchalantly in his pockets but leaning towards her slightly in a half-protective, half-menacing manner.

"I could kill him," Jack breathed in an undertone, as Alison linked her arm through his and gently guided him away.

"I know," she said soothingly, as they walked back around the corner towards the main playground. "But it really wouldn't be worth it, Jack. Do you want to get yourself into any more trouble? And especially on account of him?"

That reminded Jack of Mrs. Grimshaw's letter and her signature at the bottom of it. He eagerly relayed this to Alison, who listened with wide-eyed astonishment.

"Wow! I must admit I've never liked her all that much – she's always so cold and stern. But this is something else. You think she might be part of the Dark?"

"It looks like it," Jack replied. "But we've got no proof."

Not for the first time, they were at a loss as to what they should do next. The morning bell sounded.

"Meet me at break time," Alison suggested, as they made their way towards the entrance.

"Where?"

She shrugged. "The library? Seems the obvious place. If we're going to find out anything more, it's most likely going to be there."

"OK." Jack did not have any better ideas.

The first lesson, geography, passed uneventfully. Jack tried to concentrate on strip farming in the Peruvian Andes, but it was very difficult to muster any interest in the agricultural life of a distant country when he had an ever-deepening and darkening mystery to solve on his own doorstep.

Morning break found Jack and Alison in the library. It was deserted except for the bustling figure of Miss Batstone rearranging and tidying the shelves.

"Hello, dears," she beamed, peering at them short-sightedly over her glasses, which were perched quizzically in their usual fashion on the end of her nose. "Were you looking for anything in particular?"

"Er – South American agriculture," Jack replied quickly. "I've got an essay to write on farming in the Andes."

"Come over here, dear," Miss Batstone chirped brightly, indicating a row of shelves in the far corner, and began busying herself rummaging through the books. Jack followed, trying to feign interest, while Alison scanned the shelves for any clues or shadowy signs. There appeared to be nothing untoward.

"Now, let me see – Amazonian Ecosystems – Salt Mining in Bolivia – ah, here we are, Andean Agriculture." Miss Batstone lovingly plucked a volume from the shelf, and carried it over to her desk, cradled in her plump arms. She duly stamped it and handed it to Jack with much the same pride and care that a new mother might pass her baby to an admirer to hold and marvel at.

"Thanks, miss."

There appeared to be no reason to stay, so surveying the large room one final time, Jack and Alison headed back out into the corridor. Neither of them knew what they had expected to find, but it was with a sense of disappointment that they trudged towards the main entrance in silence, each wondering how they were ever going to get to the bottom of the sinister goings-on within the school.

A tall figure ahead was striding towards them. Alison nudged Jack and hissed, "It's Grimshaw."

The deputy head teacher swept past them, inclining her head slightly in a frosty nod.

"Where d'you reckon she's going?" Alison whispered.

"Dunno. Let's follow her and see."

Alison looked doubtful. "The bell will be going any minute now."

"Who cares! Do you want to find out what she's up to, or not?"

They waited a minute, until Mrs. Grimshaw had retreated around a corner, then turned and retraced their steps, taking care to maintain a safe distance behind her so they would not be detected. Less than five minutes later they were back in the corridor which led to the library and there was no sign of Mrs. Grimshaw. The corridor which stretched some fifty metres ahead was deserted.

"Where's she gone?" Alison mused, with a puzzled frown. "We weren't that far behind her."

The pair stood irresolutely for a moment. Just as Jack was beginning to wonder whether the detestable deputy head teacher actually *was* a witch, and had the ability to vanish into thin air, he heard a murmur of low voices coming from somewhere to the left. Alison had evidently heard them too, and was creeping stealthily forward in their direction. Jack followed, and they stopped outside the library door. The voices were definitely coming from inside the room, and after a swift glance around to ensure nobody else was in the vicinity, they pressed their ears to the door, listening intently. Two female voices were discernible, one high-pitched and somewhat agitated in tone, the other lower, cold and measured. Their words could not be heard behind the door, but the voices were unmistakably those of Miss Batstone and Mrs. Grimshaw. They sounded as though they were locked in an altercation; Miss Batstone's voice became increasingly shrill, while the latter's, although controlled, was slightly raised and hostile in tone. Both Jack and Alison strained to hear what the librarian and deputy head were discussing, but to no avail.

Footsteps approaching the door informed them that the interchange had ended. Jack seized Alison's arm and they dashed to the classroom opposite. He cautiously turned the handle and pushed the door open. Thankfully, the room was empty. He and Alison ran inside, just as the library door opened, and out stumbled Miss Batstone, her face flushed and her eyes moist. She shuffled along the corridor, sniffing and dabbing her eyes with a tissue.

Minutes passed, and still there was no sign of Mrs. Grimshaw. The ticking of the clock on the wall seemed interminable. What on earth could she be doing in there? What dark secrets was she burying or unearthing? They crouched noiselessly behind the door, leaving it slightly ajar so they could peer out without being seen.

Eventually, the library door opened again, and Mrs. Grimshaw stepped out, her face set like cement but, unusually, her eyes blazing with a ferocity Jack had never seen before. She turned sharply and strode down the corridor. Jack and Alison held their breath as they listened to the heavy, measured footsteps retreating and finally dying away. They waited two or three more minutes before gingerly pushing the classroom door open, scanning the empty corridor and then diving into the library opposite. Wordlessly, they looked around. The room appeared to be no different than when they had last examined it barely half an hour earlier. The neatly stacked shelves stood undisturbed, each book in its allotted place. Alison finally found her tongue.

"What do you think was going on in here between Grimshaw and the Old Bat? She looked really upset when she came out – Old Batty, I mean. What on earth could Grimshaw have said to her?"

"I don't know," Jack replied slowly. "But did you see Grimshaw's face? Her eyes – they looked positively evil!"

The pair fell silent again, their eyes searching vainly around the room for some sign, some clue – anything. They both felt compelled to stay, although there seemed to be no logical reason for doing so.

"Jack," Alison said suddenly, wrinkling her nose, "can you smell something?"

Jack sniffed the air. There was always a faintly musty odour in the library, but now that he was concentrating on it, he thought he could detect another indistinct but vaguely familiar smell. He stood there, sniffing and frowning. Alison would have found the sight quite comical were it not for the gravity of the situation. Jack felt a chill creeping up his spine. The smell was not strong but it was now unmistakable.

"I can smell it," he said. "And I've smelt it before – only it was much stronger then – when that demon was in here before.

Something must have been going on in here. The Darkness has been back – whatever – or whoever – it is."

"I wonder whereabouts it's coming from?" Alison pondered, trying to control the growing nausea she felt at the mention of her first demonic assault. She set off around the room like a hound chasing the fox's scent, stopping abruptly by a bookcase in the corner of the library a few minutes later.

"I think it's stronger over here." Alison wrinkled her nose again and perused the shelves in front of her. Jack walked across to join her, past the history section, then religion and philosophy. The shelf in front of them was half empty. Alison was right; the odour did seem more intense here.

"What section's this?" he asked. "It's not marked." Every other case was neatly labelled to indicate its subject matter; this one had none. Jack had never paid much attention to the books in the library before; in fact, prior to the last few weeks he had scarcely set foot there.

"I don't know," Alison muttered, and began looking through the sparse contents of the shelf. "There's a book on Egyptian gods, something on Greek mythology—"

"There's something missing," Jack noticed suddenly, pointing to a gap between two volumes. He leant forward for a closer look. Was it his imagination, or was the space which should have been occupied by a book unusually dark? He surveyed the shelves, trying to ascertain to what extent shadows were cast by the light from the windows. This did seem unnaturally dark. Alison followed his gaze and bent towards the shelf. She instantly recoiled, grimacing.

"Ugh! It stinks! *That's* where the smell is coming from."

"Are you sure?" Jack knelt on the floor, and tentatively sniffed in the direction of the vacant space. She was right; there was a sulphurous odour emanating from it. And it definitely resembled the stench of the demons they had previously encountered, albeit less pungent. Had one of those creatures been back here again? Or had whatever book occupying that space left the odorous dark recess behind? If so, what did the book contain, and who had removed it? And what did it have to do with the interchange he and Alison had just semi-witnessed between Mrs. Grimshaw and Miss Batstone? Jack was certain that had been no coincidence; the two events were somehow connected. They had to be. His mind whirled with possibilities.

"Alison, were either Grimshaw or the Old Bat carrying anything when they came out of here?"

Alison frowned in concentration. "No," she replied thoughtfully, "they both came out empty-handed; I'm sure of it. Old Batty was crying into her hanky, but she wasn't holding anything else. And Grimshaw was marching up the corridor like a Sergeant Major, the way she does, with her arms swinging down by her sides. I'm sure she wasn't carrying anything. Why? What are you thinking?"

"I'm thinking that whatever book was on this shelf has got something to do with all of this, and I'm wondering who has taken it out of here and why?"

"And you think either Grimshaw or Old Batty might have it?"

"It would make sense. Whatever was going on between them must have something to do with all of this." Jack's mind was working fast. "Think about it. We came in here earlier and didn't find anything. We've come in again and found a dark shadow and a pong where a book ought to be. And in between, Grimshaw's come storming in here and had a right go at the Old Bat. What if she was after the book? Batstone's the only person who knows every book in this library. She loves her books. Whatever Grimshaw was saying to her obviously really upset her. What if Grimshaw was trying to force her to give her it?"

Alison nodded slowly. "That does make sense. Except that – where is the book? If neither of them took it out just now, then who did? And why?"

"I don't know, but I'm sure this is all tied up with everything that's going on. Maybe if we can find the book, it'll give us a clue as to what's at the bottom of all of this."

"Maybe. But it could be anywhere. And we don't even know what book it is. It's not a lot to go on."

"Well, it's about all we've got right now." Jack sounded determined. "And I wouldn't mind betting that Grahams and his posse have got something to do with it. They were definitely whispering about something earlier. And they seem to be trying to drag my sister into whatever it is they're up to." Jack felt a resurgence of the fear and anger that had welled up earlier at the sight of Harvey preying on Lucy in the playground. His little sister might be irritating at times, but there was no way on this earth he would stand by and allow her to be drawn into who knew what sinister goings-on. He would never forgive himself if something terrible happened to her and he had done nothing to prevent it.

Another wave of anger unexpectedly rose within him. Where was Celeste in all of this? Hadn't she promised to help them when they needed it? And yet she seemed to have vanished as suddenly as she had appeared. If ever they needed direction and a guiding hand it was now.

"So, what now?" asked Alison, not for the first time, as they both considered their latest predicament.

"We keep a close eye on Grahams and all the rest of them, and watch what they're up to," Jack asserted grimly. "And we hunt for this book – starting with them."

"And what about Grimshaw?"

Jack hesitated. Quite where she fitted into the mystery he did not know, but he was certain she was playing a key role. Could she even be masterminding the whole thing? Those initials reappeared in his mind's eye: M.A.B. A cold chill crept down his spine. Mrs. Grimshaw had always been a formidable character, capable of reducing even tough Year Eleven boys to tears on occasions. Jack had always been more than a little afraid of her. But this was on a whole new level. If his suspicions were correct she was complicit in (possibly even the instigator of) something that was positively evil. The cold chill spread from his spine across his chest, and his heart quickened. He had to face her in just two days' time. He had been trying not to think about what punishment she might inflict on him, but exclusion seemed a real possibility. Might she go even further and expel him? Just what was she capable of? Jack forced himself to push this dreadful prospect to the back of his mind and focus on the present situation.

"I guess we keep our heads down and watch our backs, but try and keep an eye on her too," was his eventual and somewhat unsatisfactory response. "What else can we do?"

13

In Search of the Missing Book

Lunchtime came and went. Jack scoured the canteen but did not see Harvey Grahams or any of his gang there. Neither did he see Lucy. He was accosted on his way out by Callum and Alfie and, acutely aware that he had spent very little time with his best friends recently, readily joined them in kicking a football around the playground. He cast his eye around the chattering groups milling around, but again, could see no sign of Grahams. Messing around with the boys and joining in their banter proved to be a welcome distraction from all the puzzles and problems that plagued him, and Jack spent a surprisingly pleasant half hour before the bell rang for afternoon lessons.

As they sauntered along the corridor to their lockers, Jack glimpsed Harvey ahead. He quickened his pace, leaving his friends lagging behind. He pretended to rummage inside his locker while watching Harvey out of the corner of his eye. Jack thought he saw him lift a large charcoal-coloured book and place it carefully in his bag, glancing surreptitiously around, as though wishing to avoid detection. Jack hurriedly found his own books and, stuffing them into his bag, followed Harvey and his other classmates to the science laboratory. Whatever book Grahams was carrying, it was certainly not their chemistry textbook. As the lesson progressed, Jack waited for an opportunity to sneak a look inside Grahams' bag. Mr. Lucas was taking an age explaining the lesson's experiment in the minutest detail. Finally, he beckoned the class to gather around to watch his demonstration.

"Jack, could you get some more test tubes from the cupboard at the back, please?" the science teacher requested. "We'll need three per pair."

"I'll help you," piped up an eager voice from beside him. Jack turned to see Marcus Littlewood's freckled face beaming up at him. "Can I be your partner this afternoon, Jack?"

"If you want." Jack sounded less than enthusiastic, but he had more important things to worry about right now. He walked slowly towards the back of the lab. Harvey's bag was slung on the floor at the end of the bench where he had been sitting. Jack glanced around: Mr. Lucas was engrossed in starting his experiment, while the rest of the class was watching intently. Marcus had already reached the equipment cupboard, and was opening it. Jack casually strolled behind the bench and stopped at Harvey's seat. His bag lay tantalizingly by his feet. No-one was looking in his direction; all eyes, Harvey's included, were on the now frothing chemicals at the front. Jack knelt down and reached for the zip. He carefully began to unfasten it, and as he did so, the corner of a thick leatherbound book was revealed. Could this be the missing book from the library? His free hand closed around it, while he tugged at the zip with the other, when...

"Could you give me a hand, Jack? Hey – what are you doing down there?"

Jack stood up abruptly, letting go of both the book and the bag. Marcus was standing in front of him, gaping, clutching a dozen test tubes. Mr. Lucas looked up from his demonstration.

"Haven't you two got those test tubes yet?" he demanded impatiently.

"Er, yes, sir, we're just coming," Jack muttered, and inwardly cursing Marcus, he grabbed some of the glass tubes from his hands and reluctantly deposited them on the front bench, Marcus trailing behind him, innocently unaware of Jack's silent fury. The opportunity had been lost, just when he had so nearly got hold of the book. If he had only been able to see the title, it might have given him some clue as to what was going on. Now it was too late.

Jack hovered at the back of the class, seething. Trust stupid, geeky Marcus to ruin everything. Why did he have to hang around him all the time? Just because he had stood up for him on that one occasion against Grahams and his cronies, now it was as though he had a hapless, witless puppy forever fawning at his heels. He forced himself to watch the rest of the demonstration and then, with extreme reluctance, joined Marcus as the class paired up to replicate the experiment.

Jack had little idea of what they were supposed to be doing, but that did not seem to matter, as Marcus busied himself arranging the equipment, chattering happily as he did so. Jack tried to conceal his frustration, and fortunately Marcus appeared unperturbed by his monosyllabic responses to the smaller boy's enthusiastic overtures. Jack kept glancing towards Harvey Grahams, bent over his own experiment, his dull features contorted in concentration. Could he sneak across and look inside his bag without either Grahams or Marcus noticing? Just as this thought was flashing through his mind, Mr. Lucas approached their bench, pausing at each pair in order to examine their progress. There was no way Jack could leave his place undetected.

The lesson dragged on, Jack desperately searching for an opportunity to go over to Harvey's bench and take another look inside his bag. But none came. Finally, as the bell rang, he threw his books morosely into his bag and flung it over his shoulder. He hung back, however, before heading for the door, waiting for Harvey to gather his belongings and lumber across the laboratory. Jack followed, his eye glued to the bag which, maddeningly, was tightly zipped, revealing nothing. He stepped into the corridor, Marcus trailing at his side, still chattering eagerly. The corridor forked; Harvey turned left towards the history classroom for his final lesson of the day. Reluctantly, Jack turned right; he had maths for his final period. He glanced briefly behind him, as though he expected Grahams to open his bag and pull out the intriguing book. But of course he did no such thing. Thankfully, Marcus also headed off to the history lesson, with a cheery, "See you later, Jack."

As Jack walked towards the school gate at the end of the day, he looked around for Harvey, Lucy and Alison, but did not see any of them. He glimpsed Marcus' spiky red hair in the playground, and quickened his step. He had had more than enough of him for one day!

Arriving home, Jack flung his bag on the floor, poured himself a glass of juice and started up the stairs to his bedroom. His mum was not back from work yet, but a light upstairs informed him his sister was at home. Halfway up the stairs Jack suddenly stopped. His heart missed a beat. A faint but unmistakable odour assaulted his nostrils. It was not strong, but was enough to make his blood run cold. A feeling of panic arose in his chest; what was that smell doing here? It was bad enough encountering it at school, but here at home? Surely, *surely*, one of these demons had not infiltrated their house? His immediate thoughts turned to his sister.

"Lucy?" Jack called anxiously. "Lucy, are you up there?"

"I'm in the bathroom."

"Are you OK?"

"Why wouldn't I be?" came a somewhat irritated retort.

Jack reached the landing. The smell seemed to be coming from Lucy's bedroom. Her door was slightly ajar. Jack crept across the landing and peered cautiously around the bedroom door. He sighed with relief; no diabolical creature was lurking inside, and at a first glance, Lucy's room looked no different than usual. He pushed the door gently, just enough to squeeze through, and cast his eyes around the bedroom for a more thorough investigation. The odour was definitely stronger, but there were no visible signs of disturbance. The pink floral duvet was spread neatly across the bed, with Lucy's childhood teddy bear seated in its usual perch on her pillow. Her books and CDs were tidily shelved, and her dressing table held its usual array of toiletries. Her school bag lay beside her desk, and seemed to cast a slight shadow across the floor. Jack knelt down to take a closer look, and reached inside the bag. He furtively rooted through the contents, and saw a folded piece of paper lying at the bottom, beneath Lucy's exercise books. Curious, he removed it, carefully unfolding it to reveal a line drawing of a woman with long flowing hair adorned with a circlet of stars, dressed in armour and holding a sword in one hand and a shield in the other.

The sheet had evidently been photocopied from a book, but did not bear its title, only the page number, 127. All that was written was the small lettering below the picture, which read, "Ashtoreth: beautiful goddess of war and fertility." But in the bottom righthand corner of the page something had been added, scrawled untidily in black biro. Jack had seen the image before, and his heart quickened: a bespectacled bat with outstretched wings, bearing the initials underneath, M.A.B.

"What on earth do you think you're doing?"

Jack started, and turned to see Lucy standing, seething, at the doorway. He had been so engrossed in the piece of paper in his hand that he had not noticed the sound of the toilet flushing and the bathroom door opening. His sister was staring at him, open-mouthed and furious.

"How dare you sneak into my room like that?" she demanded, outraged. As her eye fell upon her bag, its contents spilling on to the floor, she reddened. "Have you been going through my bag? Who do you think you are?" She was almost screaming at him now.

Suddenly, she spotted the piece of paper in his hand, and stopped, standing rooted to the spot.

"Wh-what's that you've got there? What's that piece of paper you're holding?" She tried to speak calmly, but there was unsteadiness in her voice. Her face was no longer red, but had drained of all colour.

"Good question, what *is* this?" her brother retorted, thrusting the unfolded paper towards her. "I was hoping you could enlighten me."

"Give me that!" Lucy stepped forward and grabbed at the paper Jack was waving in front of her. He snatched it away and placed it firmly behind his back. Lucy lurched towards him, livid. Then, as her blazing eyes met his penetrating gaze, she suddenly stopped, as though frozen. Her expression changed in an instant to one of horror. Jack was completely taken aback. His sister's face was ashen, her dark-rimmed eyes wide with something akin to terror. She stood immobilized, as though turned to stone, staring at Jack as if he were a ghost.

"Lucy?" he questioned, in alarm. "Lucy, are you all right?"

She did not answer, but found her feet again and slowly backed away, continuing to stare, unblinking, at Jack. He leant forward and touched her gently on the arm, intending to reassure her.

"Don't touch me!" she screamed, and there was a hint of hysteria in her voice. "Get away from me! Leave me alone!"

Jack opened his mouth to reason with her, but something in the haunted expression in her eyes prevented him. He had the most unnerving sensation that he was not looking at the face of his sister, but of some shadowy spectre inhabiting her body. He shuddered and felt a sudden impulse to escape. The pastel-pink-painted walls of her bedroom had darkened in hue, and were closing in on him. He fought the desire to close his eyes, forcing them instead to stay fixed on Lucy, and returning her fearful, hollow, unblinking stare with a firm, steady gaze. He could not put his confused and frightened feelings into any thoughts that made sense to him, but he had a strange and awful sensation that something powerful was happening between them – an invisible struggle that was both within, yet at the same time beyond the two of them. Jack could not have explained why, but he just knew in that moment he must hold Lucy's gaze; he must not break eye contact with her, however unnerving it was to look into those empty, haunted, ghost-like eyes. He felt sick to the pit of his stomach, but just knew that whatever happened, he must not fail. He moved his feet further apart and straightened his back in an effort to give himself a steadiness he did not feel. He harnessed every particle of concentration, energy and willpower he could muster from within his quivering spirit and continued to look, unblinking, into his sister's eyes.

Lucy was faltering; he could see it in the pained expression on her pale face. She was still staring at him, but her head was lowering, slowly, slowly. A shadow was passing across her forehead, obscuring her features. Jack's blood ran cold. He wanted to open his mouth and scream – or vomit – or maybe both. He wanted to shake his leaden legs and bolt down the stairs and out of the house. He even had a fleeting impulse to fling open the window and jump – anything to get out of this dark, oppressive room and away from this spectre of his sister that was anything but the Lucy he had grown up with. He did not know how much longer he could withstand it.

But Lucy buckled first. She lifted her head and fixed Jack with a final defiant glare, which she could not sustain. Her jaw dropped and she uttered a piercing scream that reverberated around the room. She took a few hesitant steps backwards, then, turning on her heel, groped for the door handle, pulled on it clumsily, and was gone.

For a moment, Jack stood transfixed, unable to process what had just happened. A wave of relief washed over him, and he felt suddenly lighter. The whole room seemed lighter too. The sensation did not last, however, as he realized that Lucy was running down the stairs and heading for the front door. Regaining control, Jack followed, stumbling down the stairs two at a time, and landing with a thud in the hallway. The door was open. He leapt through it, and without even thinking to close it behind him, ran along the path in pursuit of his sister. At the pavement he stopped and looked around. Lucy was not in sight. Puzzled, Jack made his way to the end of their street, wondering how she had disappeared so quickly. He stood at the junction, surveying the road in every direction, expecting to see his sister's retreating figure. But Lucy was nowhere to be seen.

14

Lucy's Disappearance

Jack stood there uncertainly, not knowing what to do next. Less than five minutes earlier they had been locked in a silent battle up in her bedroom; now she had vanished. Where could Lucy possibly have gone in that time? To her friend Freya's, perhaps? Freya only lived a couple of streets away, in Hyacinth Avenue, and Lucy was a regular visitor there. But surely she couldn't have arrived there that quickly? Without any clear sense of direction, Jack started towards Hyacinth Avenue, straining to see if Lucy was somewhere ahead. But there was still no sign of her. Arriving on Freya's doorstep, he hesitated. He felt somewhat foolish, but could not get rid of the uneasiness he felt. Freya's mother appeared at the door.

"Oh, hello, Jack. Can I help you?"

"Er, hi, Mrs. Wright. I was just wondering whether Lucy was there?"

"No, she isn't." Freya's mother looked a little worried, and called up the stairs to her daughter.

"Freya, love? Have you seen Lucy this afternoon? Jack's here looking for her."

"No, I haven't seen her since we finished school."

"OK, not to worry. She's probably back home by now. Thanks, anyway," Jack muttered hurriedly, and turning away from Mrs. Wright's quizzical look, he ran back down the path and along the road. There seemed little point in searching anywhere else; he had no idea where she could be. Perplexed, Jack headed back home, not knowing what else to do. As he turned back into his own street he saw that his front door stood wide open, where he had left in such haste. Fortunately his mum's car had not yet appeared in the drive, so at least he would not have to try and explain that to her.

Jack was overcome with a sudden exhaustion. It had taken all the energy, willpower and self-control he possessed to withstand that unearthly encounter with Lucy. Whatever had happened between them had been undeniably powerful, and he now felt drained. He stepped back inside, closing the door firmly behind him.

"Hi, Jack."

He jumped, startled.

"Lucy? Oh, hi – it's you. What are you doing here?"

Alison stood in the hallway, looking slightly abashed.

"I rang the bell, but there was no answer, and the door was wide open," she explained apologetically.

"Oh, yeah. Right."

"What's going on?"

"Long story."

Jack sank to the floor, knees raised to his chest.

"Are you all right? You look terrible." Alison moved closer and sat on the bottom stair beside him.

"No, not really." His mind was reeling. "Something really weird has just happened."

"Go on," Alison said gently, and waited for Jack to collect his thoughts and recount the afternoon's events as best he could. He found it hard to describe the altercation in Lucy's bedroom, but Alison listened patiently.

Jack finally finished, and a silence descended. He felt drained of all energy and emotion, except for the disquiet that gnawed at the pit of his stomach. Alison was hesitant to speak.

"Jack," she faltered at last, "I don't want to worry you more, but I came over to tell you what I've just found out, about an hour ago."

"What is it?"

"When I was leaving school, I saw the two Year Ten girls hanging around the gate. They were obviously waiting for someone."

"Grahams?" Jack interrupted.

Alison shook her head. "I didn't see him. But another boy looked as if he was walking up to them. They didn't say anything, just walked off, and he followed them, out of the gate. I don't know who he is, but I'm sure he was part of the group I saw in the library last week. So I followed at a bit of a distance, so it wouldn't look obvious. The boy caught up with them, and they were so busy whispering together, I don't think they even knew I was behind them."

"Did you hear anything? What were they talking about?"

"I don't know." Alison frowned. "I wasn't close enough to hear anything. But they looked pretty intense – they were obviously discussing something important. I saw the tall girl fishing in her bag and taking something out."

"What was it?" Jack broke in eagerly.

"I didn't see." Alison frowned again. "They went around a corner just at that moment. And at the same time, some boy was coming around from the opposite side, and crashed right into them. I think he's in your year, Jack – spiky ginger hair and glasses?"

"Marcus Littlewood," Jack groaned. Typical Marcus, careering in where he was not wanted and causing chaos.

"Well, anyway," continued Alison, "there was a bit of aggro and a lot of apologizing from – Marcus, you said – and he ran straight past me, looking dead embarrassed. I waited a couple of minutes and then carried on. They were quite a way ahead by then, but I found this lying on the ground, just around the corner."

As she spoke, she handed Jack a small, crumpled piece of paper. "I'm guessing one of them must have dropped this when that other boy ran into them."

Jack took the paper and straightened it. He had an uncanny feeling he knew what he was going to find, so was not entirely surprised to be confronted with another bespectacled vampire bat untidily scrawled in black biro. But this time, something had been written underneath in a more careful, deliberate hand:

2NITE:12.00LBY

"Tonight at twelve – midnight!" Jack exclaimed.

"Exactly. They're up to something, and whatever it is, they're going to do it at midnight tonight in the library. What else could it mean?"

Jack nodded, thinking hard. The two girls and the boy had evidently been passing a message to each other; had it circulated around the whole gang? Who had instigated it? And how was Lucy mixed up in it all? His earlier queasiness resurfaced.

Jack was dimly aware of a car pulling on to the drive, and a minute or two later his mother stepped into the hallway.

"Hello, Jack," she began brightly, then, seeing Alison sitting on the stairs, her expression changed to one of surprise and then, hastily, of welcome.

"Oh, hello, Alison. How are you?"

"Fine, thank you, Mrs. Fletcher."

There was a moment's awkward silence.

"Lucy just texted me to say she's at Freya's," Jack's mum continued breezily. "Would you like to stay for dinner, Alison? Do you like risotto? I've got plenty, as Lucy won't be here."

Alison exchanged a brief, nervous glance with Jack. He nodded. She might as well stay; it would give them longer to figure out what to do next. There was no point adding to his mother's concern by informing her that Lucy was not at Freya's and he had no idea where she was or what she was up to.

"That would be lovely, thank you, Mrs. Fletcher," Alison answered politely. "I'll just phone my mum to let her know."

They retreated into the living room, while Jack's mum busied herself in the kitchen, murmuring in low voices to ensure that they could not be overheard.

"So, we need to follow them tonight," Jack began. "Whatever it is they're up to, we need to go down to school for midnight, and find out what's going on."

Alison nodded her assent. What else was there to do?

"Does the name 'Ashtoreth' mean anything to you?" Jack enquired, thinking back to the piece of paper he had discovered earlier in Lucy's bag. He retrieved it from his pocket and looked at it again.

"No, I've never heard of it," Alison replied. "We could google it."

"Good idea." Jack grabbed the laptop from the sideboard and began tapping keys. "Here we go… Ashtoreth…" He read from the screen, "In ancient times, Ashtoreth was the principal goddess of the Sidonians or Phoenicians… She was the supreme goddess of Canaan… She was worshipped as a goddess of love, fertility and war."

Jack had no idea why Lucy had had a picture of a pagan goddess concealed in her bag, or how it might be connected to the gang's activities, but he was sure it was related in some way. Why else had she reacted in that way to his discovering it? He shuddered, as the image of her hollow, haunted eyes reappeared in his mind's eye, and her piercing scream rang again in his ears. Even a glimpse of that book in Grahams' bag might have given some indication of their intentions. He cursed Marcus afresh. As it was, he and Alison would just have to head down to school for midnight and chance their luck in uncovering the gang's sinister activities. It was not much of a plan, he had to admit, but what other choice did they have?

"Jack, could you lay the table, please?" his mum's voice called from the kitchen. "Dinner's almost ready."

"I'll give you a hand," Alison offered, springing up from the armchair and following Jack into the dining room. Sitting to dinner with Jack's mother, when neither of them had much appetite, making polite conversation, was something of an ordeal, but they got through it. Jack was quite impressed by Alison's ability to chat amiably about her family and school life, despite everything that was preoccupying them. His mother, for her part, managed to show interest without undue interrogation. He could see signs of the strain of the past week etched on her features, and felt a pang of guilt. His mum was probably dreading the following day's meeting with Mrs. Grimshaw as much as he was, but to her credit, she did not allude to it.

They were just finishing their meal when they heard the front door open and slam shut.

"Hi, Lucy; we're here in the dining room."

"Hi, Mum. Hi Ja—"

Lucy appeared at the doorway and froze when she saw Alison seated at the table. Jack was startled by the instant change in her expression to both animosity and fear.

"You're home early. Are you all right, love? You look quite pale," their mother asked in concern.

"I'm tired and I've got a bit of a headache," Lucy replied curtly. "I think I'll head straight to bed."

With that, she withdrew as quickly as she had appeared. Their mother frowned and followed her up the stairs to her bedroom. Jack and Alison exchanged perplexed looks.

"She looks dreadful," Alison mouthed, looking genuinely worried.

"I know." The nauseous feeling in the pit of Jack's stomach had returned at the sight of Lucy's gaunt face and the dark shadows encircling her eyes. If anything, she looked even worse than when she had run off a few hours earlier. Where had she been this evening? What exactly was going on? He and Alison cleared the table and loaded the dishwasher in near silence, each preoccupied with their own thoughts. Jack's mum rejoined them a few minutes later.

"I guess I ought to be going," Alison stated when they had finished. "Thank you for dinner, Mrs. Fletcher."

"You're welcome any time."

"I'll walk you home," Jack offered, glad of an excuse to leave the house for a few minutes and evade his mother's questions.

Less than fifteen minutes later they had arrived at Alison's street.

"Right then, I'll see you here in a few hours." Alison tried to speak calmly. Jack took a deep breath.

"Yeah, I'll meet you here at 11.45. Try and get a bit of sleep until then."

Alison smiled weakly. "You too."

"Bye then."

"Bye."

There was nothing more to say. Jack watched as Alison retreated down the road and disappeared through her front door. Then he turned and retraced his steps back home, wondering, with a strong sense of foreboding, what their nocturnal escapade in a few hours' time would bring.

15

The Library at Midnight

Jack did not expect to get any sleep that night. Nevertheless, he set the alarm on his mobile phone for 11.30pm as a precaution, and slipped it under his pillow so it would not be heard by either his mother or sister. He too had managed to retreat early to bed under the pretence of feeling tired, although the reality was he had wanted to avoid any awkward questions from his mum. As he lay there, he replayed the events of the last few days in his mind for the umpteenth time, hoping that something would click into place, some clue or insight he had missed that would make sense of this whole perplexing situation. But nothing came. If only Celeste would visit again and give him some direction. Or the Master. If ever he needed the peace and reassurance he had experienced in the meadow, it was now. The thoughts began to jumble and blur in his mind, and he felt his eyes growing heavier, in spite of himself.

Mrs. Grimshaw's face swam before him, her thin, pointed features taut with suppressed fury, eyes boring into his. Jack tried to turn away, to cover his eyes, to block out the terrifying, penetrating gaze. But he could not; he found he could not move a single muscle, could not even close his eyes. Her face was coming closer; any moment now that long, hooked nose would be touching his. And as her face grew nearer, it appeared to be changing, stretching somehow, so that it grew longer and even more angular. The eyes were narrowing and turning from a cold grey to a livid green. And then her hands appeared from nowhere, reaching towards him, fingers outstretched, and all the while growing longer and thinner, fingernails curled like talons. He desperately wanted to shield his face with his hands, before those claws could reach him and start tearing at his flesh, but he was paralysed. The thin, tight lips stretched across the pointed face into a terrifying leer and, parting slightly, issued a green-black trickle of saliva. She was so close now he could not only smell, but could feel, her hot, putrid breath on his face. The stench was inside his nostrils, down his throat, in his gut. She was closing in on him, slavering horribly, talons poised to strike...

Jack sat bolt upright, shaking all over. What was that noise? He realized with a start that it was his alarm, and instinctively reached under his pillow to retrieve his phone and turn it off. He must have fallen asleep after all. He cautiously peered around his room, his eyes adjusting to the darkness. There was no-one there. Had he dreamt it, then? Gingerly, he raised his hands to his face and patted it carefully. He could feel no lacerations; apart from his trembling he seemed to be unharmed.

Perhaps it had been some kind of premonition, a warning of what awaited him and Alison at school. There was no time to wonder about this now, however; he had to get moving. Jack slipped out from under the duvet and, swiftly and silently, pulled on the clothes he had left by the side of his bed. Grabbing his torch, he tiptoed out of his room and on to the landing. Here he hesitated. His sister's door was fractionally ajar; should he check whether she was there or not? He felt sure she was heading down to school tonight, but he would have liked to have known for certain. The moment this went through his mind, however, he realized how foolish it would be. In the unlikely event that Lucy was safely tucked up in bed, he could not risk disturbing her and blowing his cover, or awaking their mother, whose bedroom was only next door. So instead he crept stealthily across the landing and down the stairs, taking care to avoid the creaky step two-thirds of the way down. In the hallway he slipped on his trainers and jacket, thrust his torch into his pocket, and carefully unbolted the door.

The cold air made him gasp as he stepped into the clear, still night. He strode briskly along the lamplit streets, a pale moon looming large in the star-studded sky. Alison was already there, waiting for him at the end of her road, even though they had agreed to meet outside her house. They smiled nervously at one another, and proceeded along the deserted street ahead. They walked in silence for a few minutes, until Alison ventured to speak.

"Jack, I'm not a hundred per cent sure, but I think I saw Lucy coming this way about ten minutes ago. I had just come out of my house and got on to the pavement at the end of my path, when I saw a girl walking past the top of my road. She looked Lucy's height. She was walking quickly, with her head down, so I couldn't see her properly in the dark. But I'm pretty sure it was her."

Jack said nothing. Deep down, he had known his sister would be on her way to join the gang in whatever nocturnal activities they were embroiled in, but had not wanted to fully admit it to himself. Perhaps that was the real reason he had not checked Lucy's bedroom a few minutes earlier; he had not wanted his worst fears confirmed. Then again, maybe Alison was mistaken. She couldn't see clearly in the dark; it might have been anyone. Granted, there were unlikely to be many eleven-year-old girls out walking the streets on their own at midnight, but perhaps it was one of the older girls in the gang. Alison couldn't have been close enough to judge her height, and one of those Year Ten girls was quite short. It might have been her.

But he could not ignore the uneasy tension in his stomach, and knew this was more reliable than the improbable explanations with which he was trying to convince himself. There was no real doubt in his mind that his sister was somehow involved in all this covert activity and that she was in grave danger.

"Come on," he muttered curtly. "We'd better get a move on."

They walked side by side without speaking, their anxious footsteps the only sound on the otherwise silent streets. An occasional car drove past, but they did not meet a single soul on the paths. In what seemed very little time the squat, oblong building that was their school stood before them. Unremarkable by day, in the pale moonlight it looked more imposing, menacing even. A sudden recollection struck Jack now: an earlier sighting of his school by night, several weeks ago, right at the beginning of this inexplicable adventure. Celeste had taken him to the hill overlooking the town, where he had first glimpsed the growing shadow over the school. Now the Darkness was threatening to overpower it entirely. Could he and Alison really do anything to stop it?

"We're not doing this on our own; you know that, Jack, don't you?" Alison spoke quietly and unexpectedly, as though she had read his thoughts.

Jack started and turned to her in surprise.

"The Master will help us." Her tone was one of quiet confidence, and even in the dark Jack could see the earnestness in her blue eyes.

"I hope you're right." He wished he could speak with the same conviction, but the truth was he was more than a little disappointed that there had not been the slightest sign from the Light. He felt they were very much alone, and about to walk into a perilous situation for which they were totally unprepared and in which there was no guarantee they would emerge on the other side. It was sheer madness.

They were making their way up the narrow footpath which wound around the back of the school grounds. With no more streetlamps to light the way, they took out their torches and shone them on the uneven ground. Suddenly Alison squeezed Jack's arm.

"What's that noise?" she whispered. "Behind us?"

Jack stopped abruptly and turned around, shining his torch back along the path. He felt a momentary excitement; was Celeste following them? Come to guide them after all? But almost as instantly as it had surfaced, his glimmer of hope died. There was nothing, no-one there. The trees overhead were silhouetted against the night sky; he could just about discern the outline of the undergrowth by the flickering torchlight. Nothing else.

"It was probably just a rabbit or something," he said flatly. "Come on, let's keep going."

They reached the back gate. Of course it was padlocked, but Jack and Alison clambered over it without too much difficulty. As the pair stood facing the back of their school building they saw a sudden movement ahead. A figure emerged from behind a clump of bushes and started running towards the building. It was followed by another, and another. Jack and Alison instinctively retreated against the trees lining the field, so as to remain hidden from view. They watched as half a dozen shadowy figures stole across the field, and disappeared around the corner of the building. Jack started to follow, but Alison pulled him back.

"Wait!" she whispered urgently. "We don't want them to know we're here."

"But they'll be getting in through the side door," Jack objected. "If they lock it behind them, we'll have no way of following them." He realized he had not really considered how he and Alison were going to break in to the school without detection.

A long minute passed. Jack's impatience was rising. He could not wait a moment longer. His sister was in there; he had to do something to get in and stop the gang. Without consulting Alison he strode off, replacing his torch in his pocket, with only the security lights to guide the way. He followed the route the others had taken, Alison trailing anxiously behind him. They reached the corner and peered around it. There was no-one in sight; all was quiet. Jack crept towards the door and tried the handle. It was locked.

"What did I tell you?" he hissed. "We're too late; they've gone through and locked us out."

A chiming of bells could be heard in the distance.

"Midnight," murmured Alison. "They'll be in the library now."

"We've got to find a way in," Jack cried wildly, and began pacing up and down like a caged tiger. Suddenly, without warning, he darted back towards the footpath.

"What are you doing?"

"Back in a sec."

Alison held her breath, as Jack vanished between the trees, only to reappear a minute or two later carrying something in his hands.

"What on earth are you doing?" she demanded again. In response, Jack lifted his arms to reveal a large stone. He walked purposefully up to a low window in the corridor, an expression of grim determination on his face.

"Jack! Stop!" cried Alison, in panic. "You can't smash the window!"

"Why not? How else are we going to get in?" There was more than a hint of anger and desperation in his voice.

"You'll set off the alarm, for a start."

Jack hesitated. He was so charged with fear and fury that it was difficult to think straight. Grimshaw must have let the gang in; only a senior member of staff would have access to the keys. She would surely have deactivated the security alarm; otherwise it would be sounding now.

"It must have been switched off, or we'd be hearing it now."

"But—"

"Look, do you want to get in or not?" Jack shouted in exasperation. He drew back his arm, stone held aloft, and laughed recklessly. "Anyway, assuming we get through tonight, I'm probably going to get expelled tomorrow, so I haven't got a lot to lose, have I?"

Before Alison could open her mouth to retaliate, he had hurled the stone at the window and there was a sound of shattering glass. Then – silence. They both waited for the alarm, but it did not come.

"Excellent!" Jack ran forward and, pulling his coat sleeve over his hand, gingerly pushed his arm through the jagged hole in the window pane and felt for the fastening. He fumbled for an agonizing few minutes, trying desperately to open the window without lacerating himself. Finally, he succeeded. Alison uttered a gasp of relief.

"You'll have to give me a leg up," Jack instructed. Although the window was relatively low, it was too high to climb through unaided. "And watch the broken glass," he cautioned.

Alison nodded, standing with hands clasped tightly together, her torch tucked under her chin in an attempt to give him a little more visibility. It took a few minutes, manoeuvring awkwardly in the darkness, trying to avoid the splintered glass, but eventually Jack was inside. He flung the window open as wide as he could and leant out.

"Your turn now!"

Holding Jack's outstretched hands, Alison gritted her teeth and scrambled inexpertly up the wall. She knelt on the window sill in order to swing her legs through, and felt a shard of glass slice through her jeans.

"Are you OK?" Jack asked in alarm, as her body tensed.

"I'm fine."

She landed heavily in the corridor, lost her balance and lurched forward. Jack caught hold of her, but it was not enough to steady her, and the two of them fell and landed, sprawling, on the floor. Alison's hands rubbed against splinters of glass. Jack's elbow hit a jagged shard, while another pierced his cheek. Stinging and shaken, they unsteadily picked themselves up and examined their injuries as best they could in the torchlight. They were both sore and bleeding, but fortunately neither of them appeared to be seriously hurt. They were, however, losing precious minutes. Wordlessly, they reorientated themselves and made their way along the corridor towards the library.

Both Jack and Alison felt somewhat unnerved, walking through the school at midnight. Without the clamour of daylight hours, the deserted corridors felt eerie, stretching endlessly ahead, with only their torchlight to light their path. Although they trod lightly, their footsteps seemed to echo and reverberate across the floor. After a few minutes, Alison stopped and glanced nervously around.

"Did you hear anything, Jack?" she whispered.

"Only us!" Jack tried to sound nonchalant.

"I thought I heard footsteps behind us," Alison persisted, shining her torch along the gloomy corridor they had just crossed. Once again, the pair peered behind, holding their breath. The darkened walls stared blankly back; they did not appear to be concealing anything – or anyone.

"I think you must have imagined it. Or maybe it was our footsteps echoing behind us."

"Yeah, maybe." Alison did not sound entirely convinced, but followed Jack as he continued resolutely forward. They walked on in silence, and turned the corner which led to the library. Here they both stopped dead in their tracks.

"Jack," ventured Alison in a faltering whisper, "I'm not imagining that, am I?"

"No, you're not," he breathed slowly. "That's as real as we are."

The pair stared in horror at the sight that confronted them. The library door stood shut, wholly covered in shadow. There was no mistaking that this was a shadow of Darkness and not the mere shadows of the night, which receded into a sea of insipid greyness against this imposter. It hung there with a penetrating intensity, a faceless sentry guarding the entrance to the covert activity that lay within.

"We're going to have to get past it," Alison stated in a tone of nervous resignation. Jack nodded dumbly. There was no other choice. There was also no need for any further words.

They advanced as one, and found themselves suddenly plunged into darkness. Jack's arm flailed helplessly for a few moments as he fumbled for the door handle, at the same time trying to fight an enveloping sense of impending doom. His hand connected with the handle, and with trembling fingers he cautiously turned it and tentatively pushed open the door. He winced as it creaked on its hinge and felt Alison's sharp intake of breath beside him.

They were still engulfed in darkness and could not see a thing. They both became aware, however, of a low murmur of voices that seemed to be coming from the far end of the library. The pair instinctively crouched down and Alison slipped her arm through Jack's. They knelt there, not daring to move, scarcely daring to breathe, as the hum of voices gradually became more distinct. They did not appear to be coming any nearer; perhaps the group was too absorbed in its activity to notice the two intruders. The intensity of the Darkness was dissipating slightly and, with it, the menacing gloom that had descended on them so swiftly. Jack found the outlines of the bookshelves were beginning to emerge from the shadows, blurred and obscured at first, but gradually gaining definition. He gently disengaged his arm from Alison's and crawled on hands and knees to the nearest shelf, squatting behind it. Alison followed. From there they peered through the shadows in the direction of the voices, and could just about make out an amorphous group of figures. As their eyes adjusted further to the darkness, the figures took on distinct form, but their individual features could not be discerned. One figure appeared to be moving among the group, as though presiding over its gathering. It halted now, and stood erect and still, as though looking or listening for something. A prickling sensation crept up Jack's spine and he held his breath. The figure had broken away from the group and was now gliding through the shadows, moving slowly towards them. The earlier image of Mrs. Grimshaw's demonic visage returned with full force. He felt a strong impulse to run; even to venture back through the dark depression they had just passed seemed preferable to facing the spectre that was steadily making its way towards them. But he knew that such thoughts were futile; they had not come this far in order to retreat now. He stood up shakily, hesitated for a moment, and stepped resolutely into the aisle to meet the advancing apparition. A trembling Alison stood by his side.

The figure stopped, just metres away. Something was wrong, Jack realized; its form was shorter and stockier than Mrs. Grimshaw's tall, lean frame. Or were the shadows distorting his perceptions? It took another step towards them and leant forward.

"Who have we got here?" it mused in an undertone, and Jack sensed a leer stretching across its still featureless face. He swallowed hard and took what he hoped was a bold step forward. The figure also moved closer. Any second now he would come face to face with his deputy head teacher in her undisguised diabolical form, the moment he had been dreading. She leant a little further forward. They were almost nose to nose.

"Miss Batstone!" Alison gasped in disbelief.

Jack stared, incredulous. Alison was right; it was not Mrs. Grimshaw who stood before them, but the plump mild-mannered librarian. What on earth was she doing here in the midst of the shadows of Darkness? Was Grimshaw exerting her control over her, and using her as a pawn in her own evil machinations? His thoughts flashed back to the two of them here in the library only the day before. Her features became visible now she was standing so close to them. She was not wearing her usual tightly fitting skirt and blouse, but was draped in some kind of loose robe that covered her arms and fell to her feet, so only her face was recognizable. Her glasses were perched in their habitual position at the end of her nose, but she wore an expression that Jack could not immediately identify. An element of surprise was in it, certainly, but was it not also mingled with a certain suspicion that even bordered on fear? Whatever it was, it changed in an instant to a welcoming smile.

"How nice of you to join us!" Old Batty purred amiably. "Do come and join our little gathering. Don't be shy, my dears. Follow me." Her tone was inviting, and she gestured with her robed arms towards the group that stood further down the room. She led the way down the aisle and Jack and Alison followed obediently. The bookcases rose on either side of them like pillars marking the way. The group came more clearly into focus, seven individuals standing in a circle. A lantern had been placed in the centre which cast a dim light in the immediate area, but did little to dissipate the pervading darkness. The students remained wreathed in shadows. Jack recognized the solid frame of Harvey Grahams immediately, his square jaw outlined by the pale glow of lamplight. A nose protruded from beneath a hooded figure next to him, beside whom stood the two Year Ten girls, the taller identifiable only by her height and the silhouette of her bobbed hair, the shorter by her piercing eyes that had fixed themselves on the approaching pair. An indistinguishable person who might have been male or female stood next to them, and then a smaller, frailer-looking girl. Her face was completely obscured by the shadows, but Jack did not need the light of the lantern to confirm that his sister was standing there in the circle. The seventh figure, a tall, slim boy, stepped backwards slightly in order to make space for Jack and Alison.

"Oh no," murmured Miss Batstone in the same honeyed tone. "Our two guests aren't joining us here. I have a very special place for them. Come, my dears." She beckoned to the pair to follow her further, and there seemed little option but to acquiesce. As they walked around the circle, Jack turned towards Lucy, trying to catch her eye. It was useless; there was no penetrating the darkness that covered her from head to toe. He did notice something else, however: on the floor beside the lantern lay a large open book.

Old Batty had moved beyond the group now, and was making her way towards the back of the library. Jack and Alison could only just make out her outline, now they had passed the lantern, the only source of light in the entire room. They continued to follow the voluminous figure until she stopped abruptly and turned to face them.

"This way."

The pair hesitated. Neither of them could see any way forward in the pitch blackness.

"This way, my dears," Miss Batstone repeated, only now her tone sounded a trifle curt and more commanding. Alison stumbled forward, groping her way towards the outstretched arm, with Jack close at her heel.

"That's right, my dears, be careful that you don't trip now." Her voice had resumed its former softness. They took a few more tentative steps towards her. Suddenly, a door opened from nowhere, and without warning, Jack and Alison were seized by their shoulders and thrust forward. The next moment they were plunged into even deeper darkness, falling, grabbing hold of each other as they landed, sprawled on the hard floor. Behind them they heard the door slam heavily and a key turning in the lock.

16

Revelations

For a minute or two both Jack and Alison were too stunned to speak. They lay motionless in the darkness, trying to make sense of this latest turn of events. Then, slowly and painfully, they each raised themselves to a sitting position, rubbing their sore elbows and knees, their previous lacerations aggravated by their rough landing. Jack fumbled in his pocket for his torch and switched it on.

"I can't believe the Old Bat threw us in here!" he seethed. "Where are we, anyway?" He shone the torch around, to reveal a small store cupboard whose walls were lined with bookcases from floor to ceiling, most of which were empty and, judging by the musty smell of the confined space, had been neglected for quite some time.

"I never noticed this here before," Alison remarked, with a puzzled frown. "I always thought there was a bookcase against the back wall."

Jack tried to visualize the library in daylight hours.

"You're right," he said slowly. "The Old Bat – or somebody – must have moved it out of the way."

"But why?"

"Well, for starters, she's managed to trap us in here, hasn't she?" Jack muttered bitterly.

"Do you think she knew we were coming, then? That she was expecting us?"

Jack considered this. If, as he suspected, Miss Batstone was operating under the direction of Mrs. Grimshaw, was it possible that the deputy head teacher had been aware of their movements the whole time? The thought chilled him to the core. He knew she had been keeping a close eye on him, watching for him to take a step out of line, ever since the fateful football trial, but the possibility that she had found a way of tracking their movements filled him with real horror. They had been so careful to maintain their secrecy and avoid detection; how could Grimshaw have overheard their whispered conversations, or followed their footsteps? She must have had spies, instructed to pursue them. An awful thought struck him now, as the recollection of Mrs. Grimshaw striding along the corridor to the library came back to him. Had she known all along they were there, hiding in the classroom opposite? And had she waited until this moment to lure them to the library in the dead of the night? Perhaps it had all been an elaborate trap. It occurred to him now that it had been relatively simple for him and Alison to break in to the school and find the gang. A little too simple, in hindsight.

A noise came from the library. It sounded like some strange kind of chanting, low and scarcely audible at first, but gradually rising in volume and intensity.

"It sounds like Old Batty," Alison breathed, bewildered. "What do you suppose she's up to out there?"

"No idea. But I don't like the sound of it."

"Me neither."

The noise was growing steadily louder and more urgent. A torrent of indecipherable words poured forth.

"What's she saying?"

"I dunno. I can't make any sense of it."

Then, just as suddenly as it had started, the weird chanting stopped. There was a moment's silence, shattered by a piercing scream. Jack and Alison exchanged horrified looks. A boy's agonized cry ensued seconds after, followed by a high-pitched female shriek. The pair listened, incredulous, as four further screams rent the air, one after another. Then silence fell again. Jack and Alison were too shocked to utter a sound.

The low chanting resumed, only this time it was interspersed with a succession of shouts and shrieks, rising in volume and intensity until it reached a terrible crescendo. A deafening noise resounded, as though there had been some sort of explosion. Followed by further silence, even more sinister than before.

Jack and Alison sat like statues, mute and immobilized.

"What's going on out there?" Alison whispered hoarsely after several agonizing minutes.

Jack could not answer. His chest was so tight he wondered whether he was actually still breathing, and his throat so dry that even if he were to draw breath, he could not articulate a single word. He did not know how long they sat like that, but he could not remember time ever having passed so slowly before.

Outside, there were sounds of movement and hushed murmurings. Jack sensed an atmosphere of suppressed excitement, an awed anticipation of more to come.

A closer, gentler movement roused him. A piece of paper had been pushed underneath the cupboard door. Alison tentatively picked it up and held it between them. Jack leant forward to shine his torch on it, but found there was no need. The sheet was illuminated in the darkness so that the six words scrawled on it were clearly visible:

Don't make a sound. Follow me.

In the next instant, a key had turned in the lock, and the cupboard door was slowly opening.

For the first time since they had entered the school, Jack felt his spirits rise. Had Celeste finally come to assist them? He hesitated. How did they know they could trust their rescuer? What if it was one of the gang, or another servant of Darkness come to lure them into even greater peril? But Alison had already risen and was tiptoeing towards the open door. He stood to follow; once again, what real choice did they have? They could not stay locked in the cupboard all night if they were to defeat their foes.

Jack switched off his torch, pocketed it, and together with Alison, slipped silently through the door. A small figure stood silhouetted just outside. It beckoned to them to follow, raising a cautionary finger to its lips. Not that they needed any bidding to keep quiet; they had no desire whatsoever to draw any attention to themselves! They crept behind their unknown guide along what Jack presumed was the back wall of the library (he had become somewhat disorientated in the chaos and confusion). The figure darted nimbly behind an adjacent bookcase and halted. Alison and Jack followed suit. They stood side by side, but still their rescuer's identity remained undisclosed. Jack could see its lean physique was clad in trousers and an oversized hooded top, pulled right over its face, concealing it from view. Was it Celeste? Jack desperately hoped so; he did not really want to consider the alternatives. But if it was her, why had she not revealed herself to them?

Jack realized as they stood there that the top shelf at around their shoulder height had several books missing, creating gaps through which they could glimpse the group, just a few metres away, while remaining hidden behind the fully stocked lower shelves. He peered through the gloom, not daring to use his torch. He could just about make out the individual members of the gang, still in their circle, but now kneeling, or so it appeared. The only movement was the flapping of Old Batty's voluminous robes, as she writhed and twirled around in the centre of the group, as though engaged in some sort of frenzied dance. The incoherent chanting had continued all the while but suddenly stopped, and she stooped and lifted something from the floor. Jack strained to gain a closer look. Was it the book? No, it was something smaller, a vessel of some sort, a bowl maybe? Whatever it was, she was now holding it aloft, hands outstretched towards – what? His chin was pressed to the shelf; he could not lean any further forward without revealing their hiding place. Suddenly, without warning, Miss Batstone uttered an ear-splitting scream and flung the contents of her vessel into the air. For the first time, her words became audible.

"Come, great Marduk!" she cried. "Come, your servants await you."

An awed silence descended on the group. Jack felt a prickling sensation creeping down the nape of his neck. Beside him an elbow gently nudged his side.

"What's going on?" Alison mouthed. "Who's Marduk?"

Jack shrugged. "No idea," he mouthed back.

A deafening roar made them jump, an unfamiliar sound, more dreadful even than the discordant chanting that had so unnerved them. Old Batty dropped to her knees, head bowed, as a dense curtain of billowing shadow descended. Another presence had arrived, its form slowly taking shape within the shifting shadows. Jack sensed a tall figure rising majestically before their eyes. Was it human? Demonic? Its long-limbed body resembled human form, but it towered above the bookcases. Miss Batstone raised her head slightly and spoke in hushed, reverent tones.

"Welcome, Lord Marduk."

The shadowy giant made no visible or audible response, but stood, imperious, among its subjects. Miss Batstone slowly rose to her feet, muttering a few indecipherable words. Once again, she resumed her strange dance, and her chanting grew steadily louder, although she appeared careful not to tread too closely to the shadows which enrobed the hallowed figure.

Finally, she flung back her head and called, "And come, great Ashtoreth! Your servants await you too."

Ashtoreth! The name of the ancient goddess pictured on Lucy's photocopied page. Jack felt Alison stiffen slightly beside him, and her fingers dug into his arm.

A second explosive sound shook the room, and another figure was rising in the midst of the shadows until it stood, tall and proud, next to the being that Miss Batstone had addressed as Lord Marduk. Again, infuriatingly, Jack could not make out the details of its features, and had to content himself with imagining how the black and white line drawing had transformed into a physical, living giantess. He shuddered.

Another awed silence had descended on the group, who remained in mute homage before this newly arrived presence. It was Miss Batstone who spoke first, although her voice was now so low and tremulous that, despite his heightened senses, Jack had to strain to hear.

"The great Marduk and Ashtoreth have graced us with their presence. We are truly honoured, and bow before Your Majesties." As though to emphasize her words, she gave a clumsy, undignified bow, then turned to face the group of statuesque students and continued to speak in the same tremulous tone.

"And now, we have but one more deity to invoke, the greatest and most powerful of them all. You have all played your part and given your contribution. But now the final offering is required, which only one of you has been chosen to give. Only the blood of the purest and most innocent among you will bring him to us."

She had no sooner uttered these enigmatic words when a cloud appeared from nowhere and, swirling about the circle, enveloped the group in a dense and darkening fog, until nothing remained visible. Jack blinked hard several times, but it made no difference. They were shrouded in total, terrible darkness. He listened intently to the noises within the fog, an indication that some activity was taking place. The shuffling of feet. A harsh, scraping sound, as though something heavy was being dragged across the floor. A girl's muffled scream. More scuffing and shuffling. Followed by silence once more.

Now the density of the fog seemed to dissipate just a little, just enough for Jack and Alison to discern the indistinct shapes that constituted the group. They appeared to be standing back in their original circle, but now something else had been placed in the centre, a large object, unrecognizable in the gloom. A figure, presumably Miss Batstone, stood beside it. There was a deathly hush, broken finally by the figure, revealing herself indeed as the batty librarian.

"And now, at last, all our preparations are complete." With barely suppressed excitement, her voice rose to another level of high-pitched intensity. "Come, great and powerful Baal. Come, your servants await your mighty presence!"

In the midst of the swirling cloud, the Old Bat's silhouetted frame straightened. Head thrown back, arms outstretched, the loose sleeves of her gown flapped like the wings of a bird.

No. Like the wings of a bat.

A vampire bat.

Marduk. Ashtoreth. Baal.

M.A.B.

17

The Darkness Deepens

The untidy drawing of the bespectacled bat with the three initials scrawled underneath flashed through Jack's mind. He baulked, as though struck by a bolt of lightning, and stared, mesmerized, at the diminutive robed figure who no longer bore any resemblance to the plump, affable librarian, but had transformed into a priestess of the Dark deities she had invoked. It was still difficult to make out exactly what was happening, but the fog did seem to be gradually clearing. As the scene slowly unfolded before his bewildered eyes, he realized one of the students was missing from the circle. He counted to make sure: yes, there were only six crouched figures. Where was the seventh? His eyes were drawn back to the object in the centre of the circle. It was long and narrow, a bench perhaps, or maybe a low table? Why had it been placed there? As he looked more closely, Jack saw that it was not empty. There was something lying on top of it.

Something? Or *someone?*

His stomach lurched as he recognized that the motionless shape was that of a human body. A small, slender human body. Why was it lying so still? Was it dead? Something clicked in his brain, and Jack looked around wildly, panic seizing him. Which of the students was missing? Which one was lying there, helpless and defenceless? He desperately scanned the kneeling figures encircling their prostrate companion, but it was impossible to differentiate one from another, kneeling as they were with heads bowed, still shrouded in shadow. The cloud that surrounded them seemed to be seeping into his mind; his senses started to feel foggy, and there was a dull thudding somewhere in the back of his head. A glint of something metallic focussed his attention back to Miss Batstone. She was standing beside the bench (or whatever it was), facing the prone body. The pounding in his head intensified, and everything seemed to shift into slow motion. Miss Batstone was holding something in both hands, which she was lifting slowly, excruciatingly slowly, until she stood motionless, arms raised above her head, holding the glittering object aloft.

It was a knife.

In an instant, everything came sharply into focus, as the realization hit him with full force. He had heard the agonized screams of each of the students as, one by one, they gave their 'contribution' – drops of their own blood, which the depraved librarian had offered up in order to invoke the deities of Darkness. And now the final offering was the victim that lay in that helpless heap, the blade of the knife hovering over it. This sacrifice was to invoke the Darkest being of them all. What had been her words? Only the purest and most innocent of them would suffice? There was only one member of the group that could possibly fit that description, the newest and most guileless recruit.

"L-u-c-y!"

He heard the shout, which shattered the silence, without registering that his own mouth had uttered it. Heedless of the consequences, Jack stumbled forward, not caring that he was disclosing their hiding place and placing himself and his comrades in further peril. He had only one thought on his mind right now, and that was to reach his sister before Miss Batstone could fulfil her plan of sacrificing her to her god.

Why were his legs moving so slowly? He was only a few metres away from Lucy, and yet it might as well have been a hundred miles, she seemed so far out of reach. It was as though invisible weights were pressing down on him, preventing him from moving forward. The blade of the knife hovered menacingly, and began its slow but sure descent. Any moment now it would reach the quivering flesh and his sister would die.

"N-o-o-o-o!" Jack screamed, and galvanizing every muscle in his body, propelled himself forward. He must reach her in time. He must.

Jack sensed an unexpected movement to the left of him as, without warning, a small hooded figure suddenly darted forward. Their unknown rescuer sprinted towards the circle, evidently encountering none of the obstacles that beset Jack. For a second the knife halted, positioned directly over the victim, just centimetres away. In that moment's hesitation the anonymous figure produced something from its pocket and hurled it towards the blade. There was a sound of steel hitting steel, followed by an explosion of light.

It all happened in an instant. The heaviness Jack had experienced lifted, and he felt himself falling, weightless, to the floor. He looked up, but the light was blinding and he could not see a thing. The circle, the bench, Miss Batstone, the knife, had all disappeared from view. Cries of fear and confusion reverberated. Jack closed his eyes to shield them from the glare, and buried his face in his hands.

Several moments passed, and amidst the noise and commotion Jack became aware of another sensation; a familiar unpleasant odour had crept into his nostrils. He opened his eyes and pulled himself up to a sitting position. The light was still very bright after the gloom of the darkness, but it was not quite as dazzling as before, and Jack could see a little. As his eyes slowly adjusted to the contrasting light, he surveyed the scene before him with more clarity. In the centre of the room stood a bench, and bound to it with ropes was indeed his sister. He could not see her face, lying supine as she was, and garbed in a long white robe, but it was unmistakably Lucy. Miss Batstone remained standing beside her, an expression of mingled anguish, fury and disbelief etched across her contorted features, as the final execution of her plan had been thwarted so unexpectedly. The circle had broken, as the rest of the gang had backed themselves into corners and crevices, behind bookcases, underneath tables. A cursory glance revealed the fear on their wan faces. Into their place had stepped the unidentified rescuer, who now stood facing a speechless Miss Batstone across the bench. Behind them, towering above the bookcases, heads almost touching the ceiling, were the vast and terrible figures of Marduk and Ashtoreth. Side by side, silent and still like two pillars of stone, they stood in condescending majesty, presiding over the chaotic group below.

The male deity was robed in an elaborate garment which fell to his feet, deep crimson intricately decorated with intertwining circles of silver and gold. A tall, ornate crown accentuated his great height, below which a pair of thick eyebrows were set in a permanent frown. A bushy moustache and long, knotted beard meant that the only visible facial feature was a pair of piercing green eyes, glaring unblinkingly at the scene below. In his monstrously large hands he wielded a hefty unfamiliar weapon, more akin to a spade than a sword. Curled around his feet was a long scaly creature, which appeared to have the body of a snake but the head and claws of a dragon.

Beside Marduk stood the goddess Ashtoreth, beautiful but dreadful. Her hair cascaded below her shoulders in wild ebony waves and her dark eyes flashed haughtily, her scarlet lips pursed together, merciless and proud. She was crowned with a golden circlet of stars, just as the line drawing had shown, and wore long, flowing robes of purple, gold and blue, embroidered with moons and stars. Her hands also held the sword and shield depicted in the picture.

Alison was similarly trying to process the scene that met their eyes. They both sensed there was more activity to come;

the sulphurous smell was growing, and already shadows were re-forming in the corners of the room. Lucy might have been saved from slaughter by Miss Batstone's knife, but she was not out of danger yet. Nor were any of them. Without pausing for further thought, Jack ran towards his sister. Her body was trembling violently, but the abject terror he saw in her face when his eyes met hers nearly sent him reeling. He steadied himself against the bench to which she was tied, and winced as he noticed how the ropes binding her cut into her flesh.

"It's OK, Lucy," he murmured, placing his hand gently on her quivering arm, in an attempt to reassure her. "You're OK now. I'm going to get you out of here."

She did not respond, and for one awful moment Jack wondered whether he was too late and that she was already dead. He could not contemplate the prospect, and looked desperately around for something with which he could free her. A glint of metal caught his eye; the knife lay where it had fallen, just metres away from his feet. He dived towards it but Miss Batstone, anticipating his action, swooped down and grasped the handle with a deftness of which he would never have believed her capable. She straightened up to face Jack, the knife clutched to her chest, her lips stretching into a twisted smile.

"Not so fast," she hissed.

Jack instinctively stepped back against the bench to shield his sister from the advancing foe. She lunged towards him with a murderous look in her eyes, knife outstretched. There was nowhere to escape without abandoning Lucy to her terrible fate. Jack tried to control the rising panic in his stomach, but the situation was hopeless. He had no weapon with which to defend them or attack, and there was no way out. He could feel Miss Batstone's repugnant breath as, panting like a hound poised for the kill, she prepared for her final fatal blow. But the Old Bat's breath was not all he could sense. The sulphurous odour had intensified all the while, and the shadows that had begun as amorphous shades of grey in the corners and recesses of the library had now emerged as fully-formed demons. They too were advancing behind Miss Batstone, row upon row of hideous slavering creatures, with ferocious slanted eyes and bared teeth. There was a whole army of them, Jack realized with sudden horror. A whole army, moving as one. And at the head was an exultant Miss Batstone, her knife poised to strike, a mere arm-length away. In moments it would all be over. Never had Jack felt so utterly hopelessly and helplessly alone. He could not save himself. He could not save his sister. He could not save his friend.

His friend. Where was Alison? And the mysterious hooded figure? And where, oh where, was Celeste when he most needed her, in his last desperate moments of life?

Where was the Master?

The Master.

The metallic blade was plunging towards his chest, its sharpened point aiming straight for his heart. There was nothing he could do to prevent its sure descent. Nothing.

"H-e-l-p!"

His final modicum of strength was concentrated in the anguished plea which escaped, strangled and desperate, from somewhere within his tightened throat.

The blade had arrived. Jack closed his eyes and a searing pain tore through his chest. The end had finally come.

18

Unexpected Interventions

Jack became dimly aware he was lying flat on his back, bathed in warmth and light. Where was he? Could he be in heaven? He had felt the knife piercing his heart, so he surely must be dead. Slowly he opened his eyes to discover a haze surrounding him; not the blinding light of earlier, but a soft glow, rather like the early morning mist. He felt strangely peaceful. Gingerly, Jack moved his arms and, surprised to feel no pain, gently eased into a sitting position. What had happened? He glanced nervously down at his chest, expecting to find a gaping wound gushing with blood. But there was nothing. No trace of blood or injury. How could that be? He must be dreaming or, as he had first suspected, he had died and entered another life.

Jack looked around him and through the haze saw a stout, statuesque figure. A few metres to the left stood another, more slender. A low bench stood between them, the outline of a supine body clearly visible. So, he was still in the library. He had not gone to heaven after all. He did not know whether he felt relieved or disappointed.

But something was different. The scene before him looked just as it had before his assault, but was completely silent and motionless, as though everything had somehow been frozen mid-action. Miss Batstone stood, dumbfounded, as once again her murderous intentions had been thwarted. The hooded figure's crouched stance was suggestive of fear, but his or her features remained concealed. Even the demons, which moments before had been advancing towards him, now stood immobilized, like gargoyles, each evil face twisted with malice. Jack had the impression of watching a horror film that had been paused just as it reached its climax. He appeared to be the only person in the entire room who was able to move. He searched anxiously around for Alison, whom he had not seen since his first attempt at rescuing Lucy. The gang members were scattered throughout the library, their petrified bodies cowering in various attitudes of frozen terror. Jack passed the bulky frame of Harvey Grahams, whose face was hidden behind his hands, and a surge of anger welled up inside him. He felt a sudden impulse to strike the cowardly bully, but discovered, to his alarm, that he had no power to do so. It seemed his movements too were restricted, so that he was merely an onlooker. He could see, through the haze, the giant apparitions of Marduk and Ashtoreth, towering over the chaotic scene below them, but equally powerless to act. Jack walked slowly towards the bookcase behind which he and Alison had hidden, but she was not there. Where was she now?

The only sound to disturb the silence was his pounding heart. He no longer felt the peaceful hush that had greeted him on opening his eyes. It had been replaced by an ominous disquiet, the stillness before the storm.

Suddenly, out of nowhere, a trumpet blasted. Jack started with fright and looked around, but could see nothing. The noise was deafening, enough to wake the dead, or at least rouse the frozen figures littering the library. Another blast sounded, even louder, and the next moment the library door burst open and the room was flooded with light.

His hand shielding his eyes from the glare, Jack gaped in amazement as a line of tall figures, all clothed in dazzling white, wearing gleaming helmets and bearing glittering swords and shields, filed into the room. They stood erect, faces set like flint, marching forward as one. It was a terrifying yet welcome sight. The warrior leading the procession lifted a trumpet to its lips and sounded one further blast which quite literally shook the room. Jack saw, with delight, it was Celeste. She had finally come, and brought a small army with her. The Master had answered his cry for help in his last desperate moments.

And then there was time to wonder no longer, for the entire scene exploded into action. The demons instantaneously awoke from their supernatural stupor and leapt, hissing and snarling at the advancing Army of Light. In the blink of an eye, the room was filled with warriors and demons locked in furious combat, as a raging battle ensued. Swords lunged, claws ripped, shields flashed, teeth tore, blood spilled, and screams and howls rent the air. Jack could only stand rooted to the spot, staring in fascinated horror at the carnage unleashed before his very eyes. The deft movements and dazzling sword-work displayed by the warriors took his breath away, as he tried in vain to keep up with the speed and accuracy of their thrusts and lunges. At the same time, the demons manoeuvred with astonishing agility, one moment their lean bodies poised, ready to strike, taut with anticipation, the next hurtling through the air as they launched themselves at their opponents, limbs outstretched, eyes constricted, teeth bared, tail straight as an arrow fired from its bow. The fighting was fast and ferocious, bloody and bitter, with bodies falling on both sides. Jack searched in vain for Alison, but still could not see her, although it was difficult to see anything or anyone other than the frenzy of Dark creatures and warriors in white that filled the place. But as he scoured the room his eye fell upon another figure in the far corner he had not previously noticed, someone tall and slim and wielding a sword, but clad in grey rather than the dazzling white of the warriors. To which side did this person – if indeed it was a person – belong?

Jack was so engrossed that he did not notice a Dark creature sidling up to him. The next moment he felt a stinging blow cut into his shoulder like a whip, the sheer force of which knocked him off his feet and sent him plummeting to the floor. Caught off guard, he lay in a winded, confused heap. He gingerly lifted his head and throbbing shoulder and, gasping for breath, eased himself on to his knees.

"Jack! Get back down!"

Jack ducked, not a moment too soon, as the demon's tail swung furiously back towards him, unfurled like an angry black snake. Its pointed tip caught his cheek and a trickle of blood ran down his face. Where had that voice of warning come from? It was a boy's voice that he recognized, but could not quite place. From his crouched position he glanced sideways and could just about make out the slender hooded figure behind the grotesque frame of the demon. But something else caught his eye, something small and metallic on the floor, just beyond his reach. Jack inched himself painfully forward, crouching low in case the demon should lash out again. Wincing, his shoulder and cheek smarting, he stretched out his arm, picked up the object between his thumb and forefinger and drew it towards him. To his surprise, Jack found himself staring at a ten-centimetre-long nail. Again, it looked strangely familiar, but he could not quite think why. It was not exactly what he had hoped for, but perhaps he could use it to cut Lucy free. Its end was sharp; it might just cut through the ropes that bound her.

Jack stood with an effort and made his way towards the bench on which his sister lay captive, looking around to make sure he was not being pursued by the demon. Lucy remained in the same motionless, petrified state, her eyes wide and staring, but seemingly detached from the battle raging around her. Was she even aware of what was happening? Jack positioned the nail above the first rope around Lucy's shoulders and cautiously pushed it down, moving it backwards and forwards in a sawing action. It was painstaking work, but surprisingly effective, and within a few minutes the rope was frayed, with just one thread remaining. This was the most delicate part of the operation: how to cut that last part without injuring Lucy. He leant forward, frowning in this final concentrated effort.

"Jack! Look out! Behind you!"

The boy's voice yelled out again, and Jack whirled around to find himself face to face with the demon whose tail had struck him minutes earlier. Only this time it was not the rear end of the monster that threatened him, but outstretched talons and bared fangs. The creature lunged forward and took a swipe at Jack with its raised forearm, its bloodied claws just millimetres from Jack's throat. Jack jumped sideways to evade the advancing talons, but with his back against the bench that held his defenceless sister, he had no means of escape without leaving Lucy completely exposed.

Behind the demon, the hooded boy was moving closer. The creature let out a cry of rage as the boy seized its tail and pulled it with all his strength. It swung around again to face him, hissing and snarling. Jack felt a surge of gratitude towards the unknown boy who had deflected the demon's attention away from him, and in so doing made himself its prime target. Jack could not leave him to fight the beast alone, and edged his way around its lean body, taking care to dodge the tail which continued to flail angrily from side to side. He aimed a kick at the black flank, just as the creature was poised to pounce on the other boy. It threw the demon off balance and it swung around again, back towards Jack. The hooded boy leapt on to the creature's back and in a heroic effort grabbed hold of its ears and yanked the hideous head back. The green eyes narrowed even further until they were scarcely visible, burrowed in the wrinkled black flesh. The demon let out another roar, more deafening and enraged than the first, and the fumes issuing from its stinking breath caused Jack to retch. It began shaking its head furiously from side to side. The boy held on valiantly, but Jack could see his grip was loosening and he could not hold on much longer. He made another attempt to kick the beast in its belly, while it was distracted, but it made little difference other than to further enrage the creature. What else could he do?

"Jack! The nail!" gasped the boy, as he clung on to the demon's ears with the little strength he had left, swinging like a pendulum. "Chuck the nail at it!"

There was no time to wonder how the boy knew he had found a nail on the floor and had it in his possession. Without pausing to think, Jack retrieved the nail from his pocket and flung it into the demon's face. There followed a momentary flash of light and a howl of – was it pain? Or rage? Or even fear? It seemed to have a very strange effect on the monster, which now began thrashing around wildly in circles, roaring continually. The boy was flung off and careered towards the floor, landing heavily on his back. Jack rushed over in alarm, while the demon continued to thrash and roar uncontrollably with no apparent regard to the pair of them. It was the first opportunity he had had to see his rescuer close up, and his concern for his safety was mixed with curiosity as to his identity. In his fall his hood had slipped back a little to reveal a tuft of ginger hair, a pale, bespectacled face and a freckled nose.

It couldn't be! Surely it couldn't be?

"Marcus Littlewood!" Jack breathed, incredulous.

Of all the people Jack might have imagined coming to his aid, Marcus Littlewood was the last person on earth he would have expected.

Marcus smiled weakly, almost coyly.

"Hi, Jack."

A dozen questions leapt to Jack's mind. What was Marcus doing here? How had he got into the library, and how did he know what was happening? How had he managed to stop the Old Bat from killing Lucy? What was it he had thrown at her that seemed to have such power? But there was no time to ask any of these questions now; they were still in grave peril.

"Marcus, are you OK?" This was the most pressing question.

"Yeah, I think so," Marcus mumbled, raising himself slowly on to his elbows, a pained frown etched across his forehead.

"Take it easy," said Jack, offering his arm to assist him in sitting up.

"Thanks."

They regarded one another in silence, each with dozens of unasked questions, but both feeling awkward. Jack was acutely conscious of the debt of gratitude he owed Marcus for rescuing Alison and him, saving Lucy's life, and now endangering his own to rescue Jack from the demon's assault. All his earlier complaints and criticisms and irritations about the boy came to mind now and he felt ashamed. He glanced away, unable to look Marcus in the eye.

"It's OK, Jack." Marcus laid a gentle hand on his arm, as though sensing his thoughts.

A change in the tone of the demon's howling alerted the boys to their assailant again and they saw, in horror, that it had stopped writhing around in circles and was standing still, staring straight at them, a murderous expression in its narrowed eyes. Jack quickly helped Marcus to his feet and looked around desperately for a means of escape or defence. He realized, too late, that the advancing creature was backing them into a corner. Before either of them could even think of what to do next, the demon had leapt into the air and was hurtling towards them, snarling and slavering, tail erect, claws outstretched, ready for the kill. The force of its body sent them crashing to the floor, where they were pinned down, one clawed forearm bearing down on each of their chests, so they could scarcely breathe. The hideous face, with its green slits that served as eyes, leered at them, moving closer and closer. The huge jaws opened and black saliva oozed from the cavernous mouth where the enormous fangs stood like stalagmites. Jack felt the vomit rising from his stomach and sticking in his throat. All he could hope was that he would pass out from the stench before he felt the ripping of his flesh and his lifeblood ebbing away.

Jack could feel the creature's thumping heart against his own as it leant in even closer, its hot putrid breath on his face and neck. His own breath came in torturous gasps and splutters, but was overtaken by an agonized scream filling the air.

But it was not his own scream, nor was it Marcus'. Jack felt the claws on his chest slacken their grip and the steaming breath abate. Aware now only of his own heartbeat, Jack slowly raised his head and saw, with a shock, that the demon's own head lay lolling to the side, its black tongue flopping out of its open mouth, its narrow eyes fixed with an unseeing glassy stare. Blood, thick and black, was gushing out of the body and gathering in an oily pool just a metre away. From the base of its neck protruded a golden, gleaming sword. There was a movement and a sound of shuffling, and someone had lifted the corpse and pushed it away from them. A strong arm hooked itself under Jack's elbow, and another under Marcus', and both stunned boys were helped to their feet.

And then an even greater shock awaited Jack. As he turned gratefully towards the demon-slayer he found himself face to face, not with a dazzling warrior of Light, but with a tall, lean horribly familiar character clothed in grey, with a narrow, pointed face and hooked nose. It was none other than Mrs. Grimshaw.

19

Jack's Hardest Decision

Jack stood, dumbfounded, his relief overcome by disbelief and renewed terror as he confronted the dreaded deputy head teacher. If he had been astounded to discover Marcus as his anonymous accomplice, he was now at a total loss to comprehend how or why Mrs. Grimshaw was standing before him. He glanced sideways at his school fellow, as if for reassurance, and saw that Marcus did not seem in the least surprised. Instead, he gave their teacher one of his shy smiles.

"Thanks, miss."

Mrs. Grimshaw nodded in curt acknowledgement.

"We're not out of danger yet. Come on, there's a lot more work to be done."

And with that she briskly strode up to the bleeding corpse, grasped the hilt of the golden sword, and dislodged it from the demon's neck with one swift stroke.

Jack stared, open-mouthed. Was this really the same woman who delivered school discipline and history lessons with such dispassionate decorum? Had she actually slain a demon with a sword, and was now proposing to continue in battle? Impossible though that was to his baffled brain, she appeared to be doing exactly that. Without another word, she strode resolutely back into the fray. Marcus followed her. Jack wanted to shout out and stop him, but found he was speechless. Questions and doubts swarmed around his perturbed mind like wasps. How could she, Mrs. Grimshaw, the most feared and hated teacher in the school, be present here, fighting on the side of the Light? Surely she was an agent of Darkness, and had been all along? Yet she had evidently killed that demon and saved both his and Marcus' lives, and there she was now, alongside a warrior in white, slashing at another demon, both their swords gleaming as they flashed back and forth. The evidence was before his very eyes, but he could not bring himself to believe it. Perhaps she was some sort of double agent, and this was all an act, a trap. But then, if that was the case, why had she rescued the boys? She could have just let the demon devour them both; they would never have known. Unless she had an even worse fate planned for them? This unpleasant thought struck him forcibly and sank like a stone into the pit of his stomach, where it churned uncomfortably, refusing to settle. She fought demon after demon with formidable tenacity, Marcus close at her heels, not doing a bad job himself, Jack was astonished to see. Jack found an unwilling admiration at his teacher's unexpected skill and dexterity creeping into his consciousness, but still he could not rid himself of that nagging doubt.

By now the library was littered with fallen bodies, and the stench of mingled blood, sweat and sulphur was unbearable. Jack saw with dismay that although many black carcasses lay strewn across the floor, there were white-robed casualties too, their snowy garments stained scarlet, and their swords and shields discarded, glittering and useless, beside them. About half the demons had been slain; those remaining seemed to be fighting with even more ferocity, if that were possible. Perhaps now he might have another chance of rescuing Lucy. He made his way carefully back towards the bench, shuddering as he stepped over a smouldering corpse.

But someone else appeared to have had the same idea. Heavy steps approached from the opposite direction, laboured breaths, and Miss Batstone's ungainly frame came into view.

Her dagger was clutched tightly in her hand, and it was clear from the expression on her face that this time she did not mean to fail. She lifted her plump arms, knife held aloft, throwing back her head and raising her eyes skywards as she did so.

"Come, Great Baal!" she cried, and then her incantation followed, her words tumbling out in a discordant jumble in her desperation to invoke the final dreadful deity before the opportunity was lost.

Jack stood there uncertainly, wondering how he could stop her this time. The only option that occurred to him was to hurl himself on top of his sister to shield her from the blade and take it himself. Perhaps there was an outside chance he might be able to knock the knife out of Miss Batstone's hand before it sliced into him? Unlikely, but what else could he do?

The Old Bat's voice was rising, her words pouring out even more rapidly. The knife quivered in anticipation. Jack prepared himself to jump. Just as he was about to spring forward, he heard a furious yell behind him, and a grey-clad figure shot past, brandishing a sword. Miss Batstone's voice wavered and then halted, as she found herself face to face with Mrs. Grimshaw. The deputy head did not utter a word but, her face hard as steel, pointed her sword at the startled librarian, drew it back and then swung it towards her with perfect precision, knocking the dagger clean out of her hand and sending it clattering to the floor. Miss Batstone screamed and fell backwards, clutching her hands to her mouth. Ignoring her, Mrs. Grimshaw strode up to the bench and with three deft strokes cut the ropes that bound Lucy. Jack watched breathlessly as she leant forward and touched her on the shoulder. The steely expression softened, and with a gentleness he had never before seen in her, Mrs. Grimshaw took his sister's hand and spoke quietly to her.

"It's all right, my dear, you are safe now. Don't try to move just yet. Look, your brother is here."

She nodded to Jack, who moved obediently forward, and bent down towards his sister.

"Lucy?" His voice was shaking. "Lucy, are you OK?"

Lucy stared at him, her eyes wide with fear. She parted her lips slightly, but no sound came out.

"It's OK." Jack tried to speak more reassuringly, and placed his hand on her other shoulder. "You're OK now."

"We're going to help you sit up now," said Mrs. Grimshaw, taking charge but still speaking in the same gentle tone. "Nice and slowly now; you've had quite a shock." Together, Jack and his teacher eased the terrified girl into a sitting position. A scene of carnage confronted her, but she could not register it, could not comprehend. She just continued to stare, unseeing.

"Take her into that corner, over there," Mrs. Grimshaw instructed Jack, indicating an empty table tucked away from the fray. "Keep her calm and quiet."

Jack nodded, and linking his arm through Lucy's, gently lowered her to the floor.

"Come on, Lucy," he murmured, making every effort to keep his voice steady. "It's OK, I've got you."

She stood shakily, swaying slightly, and for a moment Jack thought she was going to collapse. He held both her shoulders, feeling them tremble beneath his touch.

"You're OK," he repeated again, wishing he could think of something better to say. He guided her to the nearby table as though she were a young child, Lucy taking small, tentative steps, meekly following her brother's lead. She sat down obediently on the chair he pulled out for her, still without speaking.

The battle was abating now, as both armies had shrunk in number, and the table was situated in an alcove which partially shielded them from the scene. Nevertheless, they were not removed from the danger, and Jack remained vigilant, while keeping a careful watch over his sister. Lucy's eyes slowly appeared to come back into focus, and her trembling lessened a little. She turned to her brother now and parted her dry lips, addressing him in a barely audible whisper.

"I'm sorry."

Her pale face was full of remorse.

And now Jack was completely lost for words. For a moment the relief at hearing her speak prevented him from registering her words. Then, seeing her stricken expression, he smiled and patted her on the arm awkwardly. The tension in her face eased slightly, and she managed the ghost of a smile in return.

Satisfied that Lucy was safe, for the moment at least, Jack found his thoughts returning to Alison. He had not seen her since his first attempted rescue of his sister, which felt like hours ago now with all that had happened since. Where was she? He had not seen any of the gang members either since the battle broke out. He guessed they were all hiding – perhaps Alison was too? He hoped she was. The only one of his school fellows whom he had seen fighting was Marcus, whose red head was still visible in the fray beside the taller figure of Mrs. Grimshaw, wielding one of the fallen warrior's swords, which was far too heavy for him but which he swung bravely nonetheless. Another demon dropped, slain, to the floor. There were not too many left now, maybe half a dozen or so.

Just then, Jack heard a sound from the other side of the alcove, mere metres away. Someone – or something – was there.

"Stay here," he whispered to Lucy. "Don't move." His words were unnecessary; she was still in a state of shock and unlikely to move anywhere. She nodded mechanically.

Jack crept to the edge of the alcove and peered around it. A bookcase stood opposite, and in the small space between the shelves and the wall sat a slumped figure. Half-hidden in the shadows, Jack could only make out its outline: knees raised, shoulders hunched, head bowed. Could it be Alison? He took a step forward then stopped, uncertain how best to proceed. As he stood there a movement caught his eye – a slow, silent movement from the other end of the bookcase. Something had been lurking in the shadows and was now stealing its way stealthily along the length of the bookcase, its lean body crouched low, its tail twitching with soundless menace. Did it know the figure was hiding there? Had it smelt him or her? The person, whoever they were, would be discovered in a minute or two and would have no chance of escaping. He had to act quickly.

Jack could see the slain body of a warrior just ahead, her sword and shield a few metres away. Jack darted towards the weapons as swiftly and lightly as he could to avoid detection from the prowling demon. Trying not to look at the dead body, he bent down to grasp the glittering sword, and was surprised at its heaviness. He lifted it with difficulty and attempted to swing it from one side to the other, with a slow, clumsy movement. Should he take the shield as well? It was even heavier and harder to carry, but he might need it when confronted by those vicious fangs and talons. He made his way back carefully, staggering under the weight of the weapons. He glanced across at the table towards Lucy, who sat as silent and still as a stone.

Jack cautiously peered around the corner of the bookcase. The creature had reached the other end, and was lowering its rear, ready to pounce, its tail still twitching. He had to act quickly. He held his breath and crept forward; it required all his effort and concentration to move soundlessly and steadily forward without losing his balance. Whatever happened, he must not let the demon hear him. He had almost reached it; the twitching tail was a mere metre in front of him, and he could hear its rasping breath. The beast seemed to be taking its time, Jack thought, savouring the moment as it surveyed its victim. He watched as it stretched out its forearm and took a playful swipe at the cowering figure below. A whimper emanated from the shadows. The odious creature was toying with its prey.

Jack leant forward carefully, so as not to topple over under the weight of his weaponry, to try and identify the person sitting huddled against the bookcase, its form obscured by the shadow of the hulking demon bearing over it. He could make out its trembling limbs and tortured breathing. Any second now, any second and the demon would pounce. Jack raised the sword above his head and held the shield in front of him. There was a slight movement from below as the figure turned his or her face towards him, suddenly aware of his presence. Jack eagerly leant further forward.

Alison?

He was not prepared for the sight that was now uncovered to him. The beast shifted its stance just enough to lift the shadow it cast, to reveal a square jaw, blunt nose and closely cropped hair.

Harvey Grahams.

Jack froze. Then a surge of anger welled up inside him and he let the sword fall to his side. He was face to face with his enemy; his opportunity for revenge had finally arrived. Why should he risk his own life in trying to save the bully who had tormented a defenceless boy and coerced an innocent girl into deadly peril? He should leave Grahams to his fate; he was only getting what he deserved. They would all be better off without him.

But as these thoughts raced through his mind he could not take his eyes off the cowering boy below. Face drained of all colour, eyes wide with fear, he barely resembled the brazen bully who swaggered his way around school. With the exception of his sister, Jack had never seen such a picture of abject terror. A hint of recognition registered in the fixed, staring eyes, and the bloodless lips moved, with difficulty.

"Jack, help me."

The words were scarcely audible, but they pierced Jack like a knife. And a different series of images flashed through his mind: Marcus, diverting the demon's attention away from Jack and thereby saving his life; Mrs. Grimshaw, slaying the beast that had been about to kill them both, and rescuing Lucy from her fate. All three lives saved by the courageous and selfless actions of others, one of whom he had been convinced was his foe.

What should he do?

All this raced through his mind in no time, yet as Jack wrestled with his conflicting emotions and desires, it seemed one of the longest and most agonizing moments of his life. But now the time for soul-searching was over; a bloodcurdling yell and the demon had sprung, the thrill of the kill gleaming in its eyes, unable to delay its gratification any longer. And in that final decisive moment, it was not Harvey Grahams, or Marcus, or Mrs. Grimshaw, or Alison, or Lucy who were foremost in his thoughts. It was not even Celeste. It was the Master. And he knew what he must do.

The monstrous beast was directly above him, limbs outstretched, head angled for the dive down to devour its prey. Jack lifted the sword and thrust it with all his might towards the fleshy underside. He missed the creature's stomach and the blade scratched its hind leg. Jack had not exerted enough force to injure the demon, but he had startled it, causing it to twist its body sideways and grind to an unceremonious halt in search of the source of its aggravation. It lowered its loathsome head, eyes narrowed, nostrils flaring, tail pounding the floor in irritation. Jack took a deep breath and steeled himself for the next assault. Without really knowing what he hoped to achieve, he ran wildly at the beast, holding the shield out in front of him, swung the sword back and hurled it forward, slashing at the first bit of flesh he came to. The creature let out a howl of pain and an ugly gash oozed blood from its flank. Emboldened by this, Jack launched himself forward again, plunging the sword into the scaly body and driving it down to open up another bloody wound.

A deafening roar followed, which only served to strengthen Jack's resolve, and he gripped his sword more tightly. It was clear, however, that he was not going to defeat the beast by merely striking its hide like this. He had to get right into its heart or throat to deliver a fatal blow. And with its thick scaly hide, razor-sharp talons, bared fangs and suffocating stench, the creature seemed impregnable.

Or was it?

Jack was filled with a fearlessness bordering on recklessness. Almost without thinking, he ran straight at the demon, blade pointing towards its eye. He did not allow himself to be distracted by the gnashing fangs but focussed solely on the sliver of livid green, its one small area of vulnerability, the chink in its armour. The beast was snarling, but Jack ignored it and continued running, sword held aloft. He aimed and plunged the blade forward, its tip piercing the membrane and ripping the soft spongy tissue beneath.

And now a truly terrible roar exploded from the creature, and it began thrashing around in an agonized half-blinded rage. Jack seized his opportunity and sprinted forward, dodging its forelegs, which were flailing furiously but futilely in the air. Ducking beneath the hideous head, which was shaking vigorously whilst emitting its dreadful screams, he crawled underneath the demon's chest, undetected. The stench was overpowering, almost suffocating, and for a moment Jack thought he would pass out. He held his breath and gritted his teeth; he would not miss this time. He must not fail. Just above him the demon's chest was rising and falling rapidly with its rasping, uneven breaths. Dropping the shield and seizing the sword with both hands, Jack stood and thrust the blade upwards with all his might. The sword sank into the undefended flesh and stuck there, with just its glittering hilt protruding. An almighty scream of pain erupted, the vibration of which sent Jack crashing to the floor, hands covering his ears. Something thick and wet landed on his neck; he looked up to see oily drops of blood falling from the wound. He had to move quickly – the demon was still writhing in agony – but at any moment it could collapse and Jack would be crushed beneath it. He could hardly breathe, enclosed as he was within the cavernous mass of hot, steaming, stinking, bleeding flesh. He pulled himself onto his hands and knees, and crawling forward as fast as he could, slid through the dark pool of blood that had already collected and was growing by the second. A narrow gap had opened just ahead where the demon had flung its head backwards and lifted its forelegs. Jack darted towards it, only to find himself thrown face down on the floor as the heaving stomach sank heavily down. He was engulfed in airless, suffocating darkness. Panic gripped him. He could not see. He could hardly breathe. All he could hear was the creature's thumping heartbeat as it fought for its life. All he could feel was the foul flesh bearing down on him, pressing down on his legs, his spine. He tried in vain to wriggle forward, to stretch his arms towards that gap which was only centimetres away but was already closing as the monster lowered its legs.

His blood was pounding inside his head and dizziness was starting to overwhelm him. He must not succumb to it or it would all be over. Jack willed himself to focus on the small chink of light just in front of him, which was narrowing by the second, but was all that was visible. It was so close, but cruelly out of reach. He was panting, but no longer knew whether the breathing was his own or the demon's, so enveloped was he in its desperate fight for survival. Either way, what little breath was left in his lungs would not last much longer. The crushing weight was pressing his ribs against the floor, so painfully he felt as though they were breaking. Or maybe it was his spine that was breaking. Or his legs. Jack could no longer tell; his body was just one excruciating collection of crushed bones, its life being slowly squeezed out of it. A wave of dizziness swam before him, and the shrinking shard of light disappeared from view. It would be a relief to allow the dizziness to take over, to transport his poor, battered, suffocated body into oblivion. The only sensation he could still just about feel was in his hands and feet. With one final concentrated effort, Jack extended his arm and with outstretched fingers groped desperately for the gap.

From somewhere above he heard another agonized cry, which thundered around the quivering flesh. This time Jack could not cover his ears and the noise shook him to the core. Then the strangest sensation: he was being propelled forward through no exertion of his own – a firm pressure on his wrists, as someone had taken hold of him and was pulling him free from the dying demon. He lay prone, eyes closed, deafened by the creature's howling, its stench still in his nostrils, its taste in his throat. The blood pounded in his head, and he gasped for breath, his chest heaving painfully and rattling every bruised bone in his body with each tortured inhalation and exhalation. Gradually, his breathing settled into some semblance of a rhythm and the dizziness abated. He felt a touch on his shoulder and winced. With an effort he lifted his head and opened his eyes. He could see nothing at first, but little by little something took shape as his eyes slowly regained their focus: someone kneeling in front of him, leaning towards him. A pair of blue eyes met his, full of anxiety. Recognition stirred in his muddled mind, dimly at first, as though he were awakening from a nightmare.

"Jack? Are you all right?"

He could only just make out the words; his hearing had not yet fully returned. But it was enough. A wave of relief washed over him and his taut muscles eased into a smile.

"Alison! You're still alive!"

"And so are you!"

"Yeah – just about!"

"Can you move?"

"I dunno. I think so."

Slowly, painfully, Jack flexed his arms, arched his back and hauled himself on to his knees. Every joint and muscle hurt, but mercifully nothing seemed to be broken. Alison had rescued him just in time.

Jack suddenly realized he could no longer hear the demon's raging and writhing. He gingerly twisted around and saw it lying motionless on the floor. A pool of blood stood a mere arm's length away. Jack shuddered as black blood cascaded down the scaly hide. Sticking out of the creature's head was a sword. It had been inexpertly thrust there, with half the blade visible, and was standing at an odd angle, but nevertheless it had had its desired effect. He turned, stunned, to Alison.

"Did you do that?"

Alison nodded, a coy smile of pride curling on her lips.

"Good job!"

"It wasn't all my doing," she murmured modestly. "You had a hand in it too."

Jack thought back to his own sword which was lodged somewhere inside the corpse. It was true. Together they had defeated the demon.

A whimpering nearby reminded him of the reason he had risked his life attacking the demon in the first place. Harvey Grahams sat cowering in the corner, slumped against the bookcase. He did not appear to have moved since Jack had last seen him, and was now staring open-mouthed at them in incredulity.

"You – you saved my life." He was addressing Jack, his words barely above a whisper, but with more than a note of awe in them. "Thank you."

Once again Jack was lost for words. It was hard to equate the trembling boy in front of him with the enemy towards whom he had felt such animosity. And hadn't he himself stood in front of Marcus in a similar position, the unworthy recipient of a perilous rescue? He leant forward and held out his hand to Harvey, who grasped it gratefully. Grimacing, for he was still shaken and sore to his core, Jack helped the heavy boy to his feet. Harvey opened his mouth to speak, but the sight of the stinking corpse, blood still flowing from its wound, was too much for him. He lurched forward and was promptly sick.

A wail sounded from somewhere near the middle of the room and Jack, leaving Alison to attend to Harvey, looked across. Mrs. Grimshaw and Miss Batstone stood facing each other, evidently in the midst of dialogue. He moved towards them, looking cautiously around as he went. To his relief, the library floor was strewn with dozens of filthy carcasses; the only remaining demon seemed to be the one that was guarding Marduk and Ashtoreth, who still stood in statuesque splendour, untouched by the bloody battle that had played out beneath them. Three warriors stood like sentries nearby, keeping a watchful eye on the prowling demon that circled its master and mistress. The rest were stationed throughout the room, their garments torn and stained, their bodies bearing the wounds of battle, but they were standing nevertheless. Jack looked anxiously towards the alcove and saw that Lucy was still sitting there, unscathed. And then his heart leapt, for seated next to her, her golden hair flowing loose beneath her helmet, was Celeste.

But now his attention was diverted back to the two characters that had taken centre stage and were engrossed in their exchange.

"It's not too late for you to turn back," Mrs. Grimshaw was saying, her voice calm and measured, but with a distinct note of urgency. "Come and join us. Come and join the Light."

"No! Never!" Miss Batstone shrieked as though she had been struck. It was a fearful sound that Jack would never forget. But there was far worse to follow.

"Mavis, please," Mrs. Grimshaw entreated. "You're not in your right mind. You've done some terrible things, but it doesn't have to stay this way. You can turn back."

"No! Get away from me! Get right away from me!" She screamed the words, backing away from the other woman, her eyes wild with fear and fury. Then, letting out an ear-piercing screech that barely sounded human, she ran, half-crazed towards the silent deities. Mrs. Grimshaw reached for her arm in one final attempt to dissuade her.

"Mavis, stop!"

Miss Batstone did stop, momentarily. She swung around and slapped the deputy head teacher full in the face. Then she threw herself on her knees at the feet of the towering giants, little heeding the snarling demon. Her arms were raised towards them, her head bowed. She was howling like a wounded animal, begging for mercy. She had failed them, but she remained their loyal servant and implored them for forgiveness. It was a pitiful sight.

Up until that moment neither Marduk nor Ashtoreth had spoken, moved or made any visible response whatsoever. Now, however, a change came over them. Anger blazed in their eyes and their haughty faces took on a stern and terrible expression. They towered over everyone in the room as it was, but now it seemed they drew themselves up even higher, their heads virtually touching the ceiling, standing proud and straight. It was as though they had finally awakened to dispense their judgement. Their lips parted and they spoke in unison, Marduk's voice harsh and deep, Ashtoreth's cold and imperious. They spoke in an unknown language, but it was clear from their tone they were unleashing their wrath on the trembling priestess who lay prostrate at their feet. It was a dreadful sight, and yet, as they stood there in all their invoked majesty and proud defiance, it was also a dramatic picture of defeat. For, for all their posturing, what real power did they have? The battle had been fought without their intervention; they had been mere mascots, figureheads.

But now something else was happening. A grey mist had appeared and was encircling the two deities, lapping at the feet of the prowling demon and slowly rising. Jack stared, mesmerized, as it enveloped the two incarnations in a thickening cloud. They were still ranting and now began swaying, caught up in the swirling mist, as though they were performing some sort of ritualistic dance. The cloud grew denser and darker, and twirled faster and faster, like a tornado. A sound like the rushing wind drowned out the incandescent voices and the pair were intertwined, spinning around as one. Miss Batstone lifted her head and let out one last anguished howl. The last view Jack had of the librarian was of her plump, grey-robed figure, head thrown back, arms spread wide, sleeves flapping loosely, as she surrendered herself to the whirling cloud. There was an almighty crash, like a thunderclap, and the entire room turned black.

Total silence fell. The darkness dissipated after several minutes, but still no-one moved or spoke. The strange spectacle they had just witnessed had brought all the gang members out of their hiding places and they all stood, terrified, alongside the others, staring at the now empty space in the centre of the room.

Finally, Alison voiced the question that was on each of their lips. "What's happened to Miss Batstone?"

"She's gone." Mrs. Grimshaw gave the answer, and there was an expression of profound sadness on her face. Another shocked silence followed. The warriors also stood, unspeaking, their faces thoughtful.

After some time, Celeste strode over to Mrs. Grimshaw and spoke softly to her. The deputy head teacher nodded, and assuming her usual air of authority, addressed the students.

"You have all been through quite an ordeal tonight, but it is over now, and we are all quite safe. You need to go home now and sleep – the messengers will escort each of you to your houses." Here she glanced back at Celeste, who was organizing her fellow warriors, allocating them a student apiece.

"You may take the day off to rest," Mrs. Grimshaw continued, "and I will see you back at school on Friday. You seven will come to my office at nine o'clock, straight after registration." The gang, including Lucy, all nodded without a word. She turned to Marcus and Alison. "You two will come to my office at eleven o'clock, during morning break." Finally she looked directly at Jack. "You and I already have an appointment with your mother later today."

Jack's jaw fell open, and Alison gasped. Was she really going to go ahead with the meeting, after all they had been through tonight? He returned her gaze, but her expression was inscrutable.

All the students except Jack and Lucy were standing beside their allotted angel. Harvey Grahams was first in line. His guardian strode to the nearest window and pushed it open with the swiftest of movements. Then, holding out his hand, he beckoned to the bewildered Harvey to follow. To the other students' astonishment, he lifted the lumbering boy up on to the ledge, jumped up after him, and the pair disappeared from view. The others followed, two by two, Alison being the last to go. She turned and looked at Jack. Neither of them said a word;

they did not need to. She took her angel's arm and together they leapt up and out of the window.

Only he and Lucy were left. Celeste came up to them, beaming.

"Ready then, you two? Shall we go?"

She turned briefly back to Mrs. Grimshaw. "You'll be all right here?"

The teacher was standing with the remaining warriors, half a dozen or so, surveying the wreckage before them: overturned tables and chairs; books scattered everywhere; slain bodies strewn throughout the room. She nodded ruefully.

"We'll be fine. We'll be here for quite some time clearing up."

Celeste took Lucy's hand in her left and Jack's in her right, and with a cheerful, "Come on then," she led them to the window and helped them up on to the ledge. They stood in a row, looking out into the night's sky. It felt strange to be connecting with the outside world again after all that had happened. Jack wondered how many hours had passed since he and Alison had broken into the school. The stars and moon shone brightly still, but perhaps the sky had lightened a little with the approaching dawn. He breathed in a lungful of air, wonderfully fresh after the putrid atmosphere of the library.

"Are you ready?" Celeste repeated. "Hold on tight, and on the count of three, jump." Jack knew what to expect, of course, but Lucy turned to her with wide, startled eyes.

"Do you trust me?"

Lucy hesitated for a moment or two, and nodded solemnly.

"Yes," she asserted. "I trust you."

They held hands tightly.

"One – two – three!"

They jumped together, and the next moment were soaring high into the air, flying, light and free. Jack gulped lungful after lungful of refreshing air and felt it cleansing him from the sulphur that still clung to him, the stench inside his nostrils and the taste in his mouth. The cool night air penetrated every pore of his body, healing, renewing him, strengthening his weakened bones, and his chest no longer hurt. He looked across at Lucy, whose pale face was transformed. She was positively glowing, her eyes alive and dancing, her entire body exhilarated with a newly discovered freedom and adventure. She gave a whoop of joy, and laughed in a way Jack had never heard before. Celeste laughed too, and Jack could not help but join them. Their laughter rang out into the still night air, as they flew above the streets, the rooftops far below. He thought back to his first flight with Celeste, when she had shown him the patches of Darkness gathering over the town. It felt like a lifetime ago. Glancing behind him, he could see the school building, with three lit windows where Mrs. Grimshaw and the remnant of Celeste's army were still working. From the outside it looked completely as it should; the ugly Dark spots were no longer there.

Now they were diving downwards, making their slow descent. The rooftops grew closer, and Jack could make out the outlines of fences and gardens. Finally, they arrived at their own street, their house just a few metres below.

"Get ready to land," Celeste instructed them. "We're almost there. Keep holding on tight and put your feet down when I tell you."

They both tightened their grip as they glided towards the ground, their garden path just ahead.

"On the count of three. One – two – three."

They skidded to a halt and Jack lurched forward. Keeping hold of Celeste's hand, he managed to steady himself and found he was standing right outside their front door. Lucy had also landed on her feet.

"That was a much better landing than your first time!" Celeste laughed. Then her expression grew serious. "I've brought you home. Now my job is done. You both need to go in and get some sleep."

Jack's stomach lurched.

"But – Celeste," he faltered. "This isn't the end, is it? We'll see you again – won't we?"

"You can count on it! This is just the beginning, but it's back over to you now. I won't be far away and I'll be keeping my eye on you both, don't you worry!"

She beamed at them, turned, and with a toss of her golden, gleaming hair, was gone.

Lucy gasped.

"Where did she go?"

"It's OK." Jack put a reassuring arm around his sister's shoulder. "We might not be able to see her, but she's still out there somewhere, and she'll come back if we ever need her. Come on, let's go in."

20

The Final Verdict

The alarm sounded and Jack awoke with a start. He was lying on his bed, fully clothed. He had not expected to sleep; his mind had been in such a whirl. But eventually the adrenalin had worked its way out of his system, and his battered body and brain had succumbed to the blissful oblivion of slumber. His all too brief respite was over, however, and he had to face the day. He eased himself to his feet and stumbled to the bathroom, sore and aching all over. He marvelled that he was not feeling worse considering the previous night's ordeal. It seemed that the flight with Celeste had somehow had a healing effect on his body, and he had emerged with relatively few injuries. Jack splashed water on his face and winced. His mum would have some questions: how could he explain the cuts and bruises that had appeared overnight?

Downstairs, she was already sitting at the breakfast table, sipping her tea. Lucy was in bed; she had a bad headache and was feeling sick, so was not going to school today.

"I don't really like leaving her here on her own," their mum mused, "but I suppose she'll call me or text if there's a problem. I've taken time off work anyway, so I can easily pop back if necessary."

This last comment was uttered somewhat reproachfully, and Jack stared down at his cereal bowl, avoiding her gaze. He was surprised to find he felt ravenous, despite the prospect of their impending meeting, and polished off his cornflakes, two slices of toast and a large glass of orange juice in next to no time.

"Jack, what have you done to your face? It's all scratched and bruised!" was the next anxious question.

"Er – I got into a bit of a fight."

"What – in the middle of the night? What on earth have you been up to?"

"I can't really go into it all right now – I'll be late for school. But I'm sure we'll talk about it later, when we see Mrs. Grimshaw."

He could tell she was not satisfied with his answer, but she sighed and said nothing. They finished their breakfast in silence, and Jack got ready to leave.

"Right, I'll see you later, Mum," he said, trying to sound cheerful, and kissed his mother on the cheek. She gave him a small, sad smile.

"Yes, see you later."

As Jack approached the school gate half an hour later, he was struck by how normal everything seemed. Students were milling around as usual in their various groups, preparing themselves for another routine day. He looked up to the first floor, towards the library. Its windows were shut, just like all the rest. No-one would have imagined that any untoward activity had taken place overnight.

At registration, however, there was an unusual buzz of excitement. Someone had tried to break into the school last night, and a window had been smashed in the ground floor corridor. The library was out of bounds. Nobody seemed exactly sure why, but by breaktime the rumour was circulating that Old Batty had left suddenly and unexpectedly.

Somehow Jack got through his first two lessons. He did not know quite what to do with himself at break. He felt strangely lonely knowing the others were all at home and he was the only student who knew the truth. He wondered how they were all feeling this morning. Alison had sent him a text message wishing him luck in his meeting later, for which he was grateful.

The morning dragged on, until the time he had been both awaiting and dreading finally arrived. He made his way to Mrs. Grimshaw's office with a heavy heart. His mother was already sitting outside, looking nervous and out of place.

"Have you been home to check on Lucy?" Jack enquired, after they had exchanged a brief and awkward greeting. "How is she?"

"She seems wiped out, but hopefully she'll feel better after a day's rest."

At precisely twelve o'clock the office door opened and Mrs. Grimshaw appeared. She smiled stiffly and extended her hand.

"Pleased to meet you, Mrs. Fletcher. I'm Margery Grimshaw. Do come in and take a seat. You too, Jack."

Jack and his mother sat down in the chairs indicated, and Mrs. Grimshaw took her seat behind her desk. Jack searched her face for any hint of what was to come, but she was giving nothing away. His mind's eye conjured up the image of the fearless warrior fighting alongside the angelic army. It seemed impossible that was the same woman who sat impassively before them now.

"Thank you for taking the time to meet with me today," she began. "I'm sure you are both aware of why we are here: to discuss Jack's recent behaviour." She paused and cleared her throat, as his mum murmured an assent. "I'm sure you will appreciate the seriousness of the incident."

"Yes, of course," Jack's mother replied. "I was shocked to receive your letter, which was the first I heard about it. And I must say that while I cannot defend my son's behaviour, I cannot understand it either. It seems totally out of character. I've known him to lose his temper at times, of course. But I've never known him to show aggression like this towards anyone, and certainly not to assault another child."

Mrs. Grimshaw listened gravely.

"I too was very surprised. There have been a number of misdemeanours of late, but nothing on this scale. I need hardly emphasize that assaulting another student is a very serious matter. I was wondering whether there were any issues at home that might have affected Jack's behaviour here at school?"

This question appeared to be addressed to both of them. Jack looked at his mother, who had flushed slightly.

"Not that I've been aware of," she answered, sounding uncomfortable. "I mean, it hasn't been easy for Jack or his sister since their father and I divorced, but that happened three years ago and we've all got through it. I've been very busy at work recently; perhaps I haven't been spending enough time with the children."

She gave Jack an apologetic look, and momentarily forgetting Mrs. Grimshaw, he reached across and squeezed her hand.

"Mum, none of this is your fault."

Mrs. Grimshaw looked from one to the other with her piercing, inscrutable gaze. Jack shifted uncomfortably in his seat and stared at the floor.

"Have you anything you wish to say, Jack?" she asked quietly.

He looked back up at her, his deputy head teacher, sitting there so coldly, so formally, as though they had not seen each other since his last interview with her and Mr. Cartwright following that fateful football trial. What on earth did she expect him to say? She had saved his and Lucy's and Marcus' lives only a few hours ago in this very building. Was she now going to dispose of him by excluding him from school? There was nothing he could say. He shook his head.

There was a long pause. Jack did not dare look at either woman. He could feel his mum's anxiety; it was palpable. He could similarly feel his teacher's penetrating gaze, those stern eyes boring into him like a drill. The silence felt interminable.

Another clearing of the throat, a sharp intake of breath, and Mrs. Grimshaw drew herself up to her full height, back straight, bony shoulders tense, head erect, her pointed chin protruding slightly. Jack swallowed. His sentence was about to be delivered. When she finally spoke, her words were calm and measured.

"These last few weeks have been highly unusual, and there have been some unprecedented events here within the school. The incident at the football trial and assault on the other student was not as it first appeared. While it looked as though Jack made a deliberate and malicious attack on another boy, that has, in actual fact, turned out not to be the case. Jack was unwittingly drawn into a situation of which he was initially unaware. We have recently discovered occult activity taking place within the school, into which a number of students have been drawn. I'm afraid your daughter Lucy was one of them, Mrs. Fletcher."

His mother uttered a gasp of horror and disbelief.

"You need not worry," Mrs. Grimshaw continued in a gentler tone. "Lucy is quite safe now. She is exhausted and it may take her some time to process what she has been through, but she will be fine. I will be speaking to her and the other students involved tomorrow. And you may rest assured the perpetrator has now left the school and will never return."

That final image of the sleeves flapping loosely like bat's wings as the grey-robed figure disappeared into the swirling cloud returned to Jack now, and he shuddered.

"Jack has in fact been one of the students involved in uncovering the activity," Mrs. Grimshaw resumed. "He and Lucy, along with several others, were here last night, and it is in no small part due to Jack's actions that your daughter and a few others have been rescued from these sinister goings-on. The incident on the football pitch, although we did not realize it at the time, was part of a wider plot, and Jack was framed for something he did not do. There was somebody else on the scene, who only Jack saw at the time. He looked like one of our students but was actually one of the agents of the Dark forces disguised as a boy. He came to test Jack, and tricked him into tackling the other boy, Harvey. It was actually this person calling himself Lucien Ferndale who assaulted Harvey, not Jack as we had thought. He disappeared immediately afterwards, as quickly as he had appeared, leaving Jack to take the blame.

"I realize that this is a lot to take in, Mrs. Fletcher, and may be hard to believe. But I can assure you that I am telling the truth. As it turns out, Jack did nothing wrong, and therefore deserves no punishment. On the contrary, I will be recommending him and his fellow students for a special head teacher's award for outstanding services to the school community. Mrs. Fletcher, your son has shown outstanding courage and integrity of character, and you should be very proud of him."

Stunned silence followed this speech. Jack could not quite believe what he had just heard. He looked timidly at Mrs. Grimshaw to see her actually smiling at him. His mother's face was a confused picture of bafflement, incredulity, relief, shock and pride. It was too much for her to absorb right now.

"You three will have much to talk about I am sure," Mrs. Grimshaw said kindly, "and I will not take up any more of your time. Thank you again, Mrs. Fletcher, for coming in today, and please do not hesitate to contact me if you would like to discuss any of this further at any time. Jack, you may return to your class now, and join me here again tomorrow at eleven o'clock with Marcus and Alison."

The interview was over. Instead of being expelled, as he had feared, he had been exonerated. He could not quite believe it. Back out in the corridor his mum turned to face him.

"Oh, Jack!" Her face was full of emotion, tears welling in her eyes. She hugged him close. At any other time he would have been mortified and would have pulled away, but such was his relief that he returned her embrace, thankful no further explanations were needed. As Mrs. Grimshaw had intimated, there would be plenty of time for them to talk, together with Lucy, in the days and weeks to come.

The rest of the day passed in a blur. Jack wondered whether the deputy head had spoken to the other teachers, as they were unusually lenient with his lack of attention. He sent Alison a quick text message at the end of the day to let her know he had not been excluded, and would see her tomorrow, and headed home. The evening passed quietly; Lucy was up, having spent most of the day in bed, but was clearly still in shock and incapable of much speech. Their mum realized this and did not press her with questions. All three were in a reflective mood, and few words were spoken during dinner. But it was possibly the most peaceful evening they had spent together in months.

The following morning Jack and Lucy walked to school together. He could tell she was worried about her meeting with Mrs. Grimshaw.

"You'll be all right," he said, giving her a playful dig in the ribs. "Believe it or not, she is actually human!"

Lucy managed a weak smile. Then, "Jack," she ventured in a small voice, "I never meant for any of this to happen. I had no idea what I was getting myself into."

"I know. It's OK. But" – his curiosity was aroused – "why did you?"

Lucy sighed.

"I was having a bit of a bad time earlier this term. I couldn't get into the netball team. I was bottom in French – Miss Strokins really had it in for me. And then Freya and I fell out. I just felt like I was rubbish at everything, and didn't have any friends. I was really missing primary school – I didn't feel like I fitted in at St. Michael's at all.

"I went to the library one lunchtime, just to get away from everyone and everything. Chloe and Bethany were in there – the two Year Ten girls in Miss Batstone's gang. I didn't know them then, of course, but I overheard them talking about this secret club they'd joined. It didn't make much sense to me, but there was something about the way they were talking that made me want to find out more. They stopped when they realized I was listening, and started whispering and writing notes to each other. That just made me even more determined to find out what they were up to. So I started hanging out in the library at lunchtimes, and they were in there quite a lot, sometimes on their own, sometimes in a bigger group, all whispering together. I know it sounds stupid, but it all sounded really mysterious and exciting, and I just wanted to be a part of it. They were all older than me, and I guess it made me feel—" Her voice trembled and she blushed with embarrassment. "It made me feel – like I was somebody." She looked away and stared miserably at the ground. Jack touched her gently on the arm.

"Go on."

Lucy took a deep breath and stared straight ahead, not meeting her brother's eye. Her lower lip was quivering.

"At first, whenever they saw me they would drop their voices and huddle together, so I couldn't hear what they were talking about. But the more I hung out in the library, the more they got used to me, just sitting in the corner, pretending to read, and they seemed not to notice me after a while and forgot to whisper. I picked up odd things they were saying: how they had each been chosen; how they were all part of a great mission; how they were going to end up ruling the school. I was intrigued; I had no idea what they were on about, but it sounded amazing, and I didn't know why but I really wanted to be in on it. I got my opportunity a couple of weeks later. I went in one breaktime, and Chloe and Bethany were in there, just the two of them. I had the feeling they'd been waiting for me, because they started talking to me straightaway. They told me they were looking for one more girl to join their gang and thought that girl was me. They invited me to come back to the library after school to meet their leader. They wouldn't tell me any more than that – it was a bit mysterious really – but I couldn't believe it. I couldn't believe that two Year Ten girls wanted me to join their gang.

"So I went back after school, and Chloe and Bethany were there again, with Miss Batstone. She was so nice to me, and seemed so pleased to see me—" Lucy broke off, blinking hard in an effort to fight back the tears. She continued, her voice faltering,

"She said – she said I was the seventh one, who would complete the circle. She told me she had a very special role for me. I know it sounds ridiculous, but it made me feel important. I felt wanted, needed even. I had no idea – I had no idea – she meant—"

She broke off again, a lump rising in her throat, and began sobbing. Jack put his arm awkwardly around her heaving shoulders.

"Of course you didn't, Lucy. How could you possibly have known? How could any of us have known? But you're safe now – she can't hurt you anymore. And it will go OK with Mrs. Grimshaw today – you'll be fine, I promise."

She did not answer, but looked up at him through her tear-filled eyes and nodded.

He did not see her again until later in the day. Harvey Grahams entered his maths lesson halfway through, and Jack wondered with what promises and lies the Old Bat had lured him into her gang. He met Jack's eyes as he walked across the room to his seat and nodded to him. His square face looked chastened and thoughtful. Whatever the deputy head had said had obviously had an effect on him.

Eleven o'clock found Jack, Marcus and Alison standing outside the deputy head's office. He was glad to see them both, and relieved that apart from a few cuts and bruises they looked relatively unscathed. Yet he found himself feeling unexpectedly shy, and did not know what to say to either of them. He was spared the embarrassment of standing there in awkward silence, however, for at that moment the door opened, and for the second time in two days Jack was ushered in.

"How are you feeling?" Mrs. Grimshaw asked, regarding each of them in turn, with genuine concern in her eyes.

"OK, thanks, miss," "Not too bad, miss," "All right, thank you, miss," came the mumbled replies. Mrs. Grimshaw nodded.

"You have been through a real ordeal, and it will take some time for you to fully recover. I want to thank each one of you; you have shown outstanding courage in the face of overwhelming danger. I don't think I need to impress upon you the power of the Dark forces we have fought against. I have spoken with the other students and I am confident they now understand the full extent of the peril they were in. I don't think any of them will be dabbling in Darkness again. Whether they will turn to the Light remains to be seen.

"We may be thankful this battle is over, the Darkness has been defeated, and our school has been saved. But don't think for one minute that this is the end." Now there was a cautionary note in her voice. "The Darkness will return. It is cunning and has many guises, as we saw with Lucien Ferndale, and it will look for a way to come back."

Suddenly her lips parted into a rare smile.

"But remember you are warriors of Light now, each one of you. Never forget to whom you belong. The Light will always shine more brightly, and will always be stronger to overcome the Darkness. So be on your guard but do not be afraid."

All three listened in silence as her words sunk in. Questions formed in their minds, but somehow it did not seem the right time to ask them. There was an unspoken understanding between them that answers would be found in due course. But for now the meeting was over and they were dismissed.

Outside the office, the trio wandered down a quiet corridor and into an empty classroom, each preoccupied with their own thoughts. They stood for several minutes in silent companionship. Outside, the clamour of students milling around during morning break was alien and seemed to belong to a different world.

Jack turned to Marcus, something puzzling him.

"Marcus, how long have you been involved in all of this?"

The smaller boy looked at him coyly.

"Not long, really. At least – not properly. I kind of knew about the Light, but – well, to be honest, I didn't think I was good enough to join it. I – I didn't think the Master would choose someone like me." His freckled face blushed.

"So, what happened?" Jack asked, intrigued.

"Well, the day of the football trial, I found that bag you dropped – the bag of nails. I didn't know what it was at first; I just knew it was important, so I kept it with me. I meant to give it back to you, Jack, but – but—" His voice trailed off.

"I know; I didn't give you a chance."

"And then a couple of days later, Mrs. Grimshaw kept me back after class and asked me to keep an eye out for you. She said she thought you were in danger and that I had been given the task to protect you."

"How did she know?"

"I don't know. I think one of the messengers must have told her. She knew there was something going on at the library on Wednesday night, and she thought you would be there. She told me all of us had a part to play and I would find the power when I needed it. I didn't really understand what she meant, but I just knew I had to go there."

"So, there *was* someone following us that night," Alison broke in. "It was you!"

"Yes."

"And that flash of light that stopped the Old Bat from killing Lucy – that was when you threw the bag of nails at her?"

"Yes."

It was all falling into place.

Jack thought back to all the times over the past few weeks that Marcus had been trailing behind him, and how exasperated he had been. And all the time he had been watching out for him, trying to protect him.

"Marcus, I owe you an apology."

"It doesn't matter, Jack. It's really not important now."

He was right. They had all been a part of something much bigger than any of them could ever imagine, and unknown to each of them, the Master had had it all in hand.

Their own misunderstandings, mistakes and failures no longer mattered.

"So – what happens now?" Alison asked after another pause.

As if in answer to her question, the bell sounded, signalling the end of breaktime.

"Well, I guess we go back to class," Jack grinned matter-of-factly. "I've got English next; what have you got?"

"Maths," Alison replied. "And – oh no – I haven't done my homework! I'm going to be in for it!"

"French," said Marcus. He looked at them both coyly. "So, I'll see you around?"

"You bet!"

And with that, they went their separate ways to their lessons.

Back to class. Back to the humdrum routine of lessons, lunchtime, football, more lessons, homework... Jack yawned. But as he sat in his usual seat at the back of the classroom, his elbow resting on the table, his copy of 'Romeo and Juliet' lying open in front of him, Miss Kirkby standing at the front discussing the feuding Montagues and Capulets, things did not seem quite the same. The classroom was bathed in a soft light. Jack's eyes strayed to the window, and there, perched on the ledge, sat a slender girl dressed in jeans and a purple hoodie, her legs swinging idly. She turned her pale face towards him now, and her long hair fell across her shoulders, gleaming like gold as the sunlight caught it. She nodded and smiled, winked, and then faded into the sunlight and was gone.

About the Author

Cath Hensby Worboys grew up in Dorset and now lives in rural north Hampshire with her husband and their two teenaged sons. Cath studied English at Royal Holloway University of London, after which she trained as an Occupational Therapist at Brunel University. She has worked for over twenty years in mental health services. In addition to reading and writing, Cath enjoys spending time with her family and friends, country walks, travel, music, and theatre. She is a member of an active local church, where she has enjoyed volunteering in a variety of roles over the years, from children's and youth work, to prayer ministry, mission, and pastoral care.

Cath came to faith as a child through reading Christian fiction (Patricia M. St John's *Treasures of the Snow*). She is passionate about the power of literature in our lives, and hopes that her writing will inspire and encourage others in their own faith journeys.

You can contact the author at:

Instagram: @cathhensbyworboys
Facebook: @cathhensbyworboys
Email: cathhensbyworboys@gmail.com

Similar Books from the Publisher

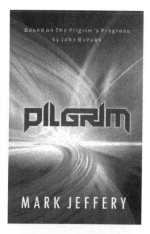

Pilgrim by Mark Jeffery

"The only hope for the people of Hamartia is that they leave the city and the planet immediately. You have been deceived. You must escape if you value your life."

After hacking into the government's computer network, Pilgrim had uncovered the shocking truth concerning the future of his city. Now his only hope was to escape from the totalitarian regime by fleeing the planet and heading for the mysterious Star System Celeste.

The Watchman of Kerioth by David Staines

There is a door that lies between the worlds of men and angels.

When orphans Joshua and Lucy are summoned by their grandfather, who has disowned them, they feel convinced that his intentions are far from charitable, Sure enough, they soon find themselves each on a dangerous quest – one in the world of angels, the other in the world of men – but who is orchestrating the events that unfold?

Books available from **onwardsandupwards.org/shop** or your local bookshop.